Bombay Sapphire
Episode 5:
Balance of Power

Created by:
Tyree Campbell

Bombay Sapphire: Balance of Power
by Tyree Campbell

All rights reserved. No part of this publication may be reproduced or transmitted in any form or by any means, electronic or mechanical, including photocopying or recording or by any information storage and retrieval systems, without expressed written consent of the author and/or artists.

All characters herein are fictitious, and any resemblance between them and actual people is strictly coincidental.

Story copyright owned by Tyree Campbell
Cover art "Rhino" by Marcia A. Borell
Cover design by Marcia Borell

First Printing, March 2024

Hiraeth Publishing
P.O. Box 1248
Tularosa, NM 88352
e-mail: hiraethsubs@yahoo.com

Visit www.hiraethsffh.com for science fiction, fantasy, horror, scifaiku, and more. While you are there, visit the Shop for books and more! **Support the small, independent press...**

Previously, in Bombay Sapphire: Episode 4:

The night air of Bhopal gave little relief.

"Are you going to blue?" whispered Atasi.

Nakushi shook her head. "I don't know. If we are discovered, they will expect to see three people, perhaps harmless. They will fear the unexpected."

Atasi laughed. "We're about to invade the Bhopal chemical plant, so you're philosophical."

"I am affected by who I may become."

"Oh, that's going to keep me awake tonight."

"Hush," said Nakushi. "I see the gate, and..."

"The two guards are lying on the ground," said Naveen. He took a couple of night shots with his camera. "Wh-what's going on?"

"Smell that?" said Nakushi.

Atasi wrinkled her nose. "That's not from the shantytown."

"It's very faint," Naveen said. "And... listen. Do you hear that?"

Nakushi keened an ear. A sound between a hiss of air and the whine of a stressed motor reached her. It seemed to be coming from the direction of the oddly-shaped tower. Clearly something was malfunctioning.

Naveen continued to shoot up night film. Nakushi nudged him and pointed toward the tower. They moved closer, to where they might observe the tower more clearly. A few lights shone, more for security than for search. A new odor reached her, this one of hot metal, as if the strain of a motor were approaching the breakdown point.

"We can't summon help from the guard shack," said Atasi. "Whatever overcame the guards will overcome us." She raised an eyebrow at Nakushi.

A flash of light blinded them. A shock wave struck them.

"*Ash*—" began Nakushi, but the explosion hammered her into darkness.

001

She thought she had a name; she was sure of that, but had no idea what it might have been. The color behind her eyelids was blue. Outside those lids, the air was thin and cold.

She thought she remembered dying.

She had not supposed that Nirvana should freeze. But then, what did she know about it?

Her head swam as she sat up. Her unfocused eyes, now open, saw harsh white light that made her head ache. She closed them again. She recalled seeing a light before she died. But not like this, not like this one. The other light had faded, along with her life. This one was everywhere and forever.

Someone had died with her. A woman. And a man with a magic box. Blinded by the light, she had not seen them. Here, she was alone.

Still, she thought she heard voices. Faint, distant, sonorous. They drew closer, and louder. She opened her eyes again.

In the glaring white light, two beings hovered, though neither had wings. They need wings to fly, she thought, and stopped. Was that true? Didn't she herself fly...? But she was unable to complete that question, and in any event the two beings held her attention.

One had six arms, a curved sword in the right middle one, and was wearing a golden stupa for a hat. The other clutched a handful of lightning bolts in his left hand; in his right, he held one ready to hurl. His head was bare, his hair long and black. Both beings were wearing great silken gowns in red, yellow, and ochre.

"She has no place here," growled Six Arms. "You should not have brought her."

"She is my *asura*," calmly replied Lightning Bearer. "My avatar. She is under my protection."

"She is *dead*. Send her away."

Lightning Bearer pointed at her. "She is *alive*," he declared.

She felt a sizzling throughout her. It damped the harsh light. Clarity stunned her. Jumbled memories flooded into her. She shut her eyes and laid back to let them sort themselves out for her.

"Let us discuss this with Brahma and Vishnu," said Lightning Bearer. No...no, she thought, that was not his name. It was...was Storm? No...Agni. Yes, he is Agni!

"Do you truly wish that?" asked... Shiva. Lord Shiva. "Will you abide by our decision?"

"I will."

The pair vanished.

And she knew: I'm on Mount Meru, the home of the gods.

* * *

A soft touch at her arm brought her around. She opened her eyes to a girl attired in a pink filmy fabric that was diaphanous above so that it revealed her girl's beginning breasts and opaque enough below to sculpt her legs without showing them. She was kneeling with legs tucked under, and holding a tray of gold that bore little gold cups filled with *pav bhaji*, dates, rice with chopped red peppers, and two different teas. About them there was not an aroma of cinnamon to be had. She gave the girl a second inspection. This was, she concluded, an *apsara*—perhaps, judging by her youthful appearance, one in training.

She selected a cup of the vegetable curry called *pav bhaji*, and a golden spoon, and thanked her. "*Sukria.*"

"Do you not wish more?"

She selected the green tea and the rice, and waved off the rest. The *apsara* vanished before her eyes. She looked for a place to set down the bowls, and found none. She seemed to be sitting on a cloud, and reasoned that if the cloud could support her, it could hold up the bowls as well. This proved out. She ate sparingly, of food that had never tasted so delicious, and drank of tea that was at once soothing and restorative. But she was Nakushi, the Unwanted One. Now she remembered. And she did not deserve such beneficence.

You are my guest here. Sup and drink.
"Yes, O Agni, but—"

I shall join you presently.

"Presently" might have meant a few moments or a few millennia. Time meant utterly nothing here. There was no time; there was only an all-encompassing nowness, in which all events were always happening. Even the realization of this made Nakushi's head swim. There was a word she might breathe, which would make everything comprehensible. Try as she might, she could not recall it to mind. She retained of it only the impression of a rich blue. Like a jewel, a *padme*. But what, what?

She, Nakushi the Unwanted, sat and waited. And waited. Time could not pass, for there was no time. Her existence consisted of sitting on the cloud. A girl was with her, attired in a pink filmy fabric and holding a tray of gold that bore little gold cups filled with *pav bhaji*, dates, rice with chopped red peppers, and two different teas. Nakushi selected bits and one by one pushed them into her mouth. Something blue was missing, but that could not be, for this was Existence, and it encompassed Everything. Agneya would know; the boy would guide her. She looked around; he had to be here somewhere, for this was All there was.

She closed her eyes, and shut out Existence. She was not ready to understand. She was someone else. But who?

* * *

In her dream Nakushi saw a great cloud of Evil. It rumbled over a city, killing all it touched. It came not from the gods, not from Shiva the Destroyer, or the wise Krishna, or Brahman, who created Existence, but from...from Man.

It rumbled over her. And over...yes, Atasi. Atasi Patel. And Naveen, who took photographs. She had been there. Or would be there. Or was there now. It was all so confusing.

In her dream, she flew. She raced past birds from the sea, and great winged things that made loud and terrible noises, and gigantic clumps of steam. Down below was Bharat, her homeland. It stretched from sea to sea, with all manner of terrain between. She had been given it to protect and defend. She had been given this duty by Agni.

She awoke from the dream, if dream it was, sweating. Air rushed past her. A chill consumed her.

What had she witnessed? Or was still witnessing? Or would witness?

Could it be stopped? Nakushi was certain, without knowing how, that Agni had shown her these, not dreams, but visions. It was his message to her. Her marching orders.

Someone sat beside her, lotused. She recognized his hair, long and black, and his multicolored silk gown.

"O Agni," she whispered, and dipped her head respectfully.

* * *

Nakushi awoke on the rocks on the shore of a vast lake.

002

Low waves of water rippled at Nakushi's feet. Out in the lake, a motorboat had passed nearby, its wake lapping at the rocks. Her body aching, she sat up. Stretching made her wince with little agonies. Eddies of memories filled her mind. At first, none of them seemed to relate to her. Slowly she recognized something of them: a person here, a place there. An adversary, huge and cruel. A man with nine fingers. A doctor, in the far north.

If he was north, then this had to be south. It felt reassuring to know that there were directions.

Several meters off to her right, a man stood at the water's edge. He flicked his fishing pole and cast out into the water. Although she saw only his profile, she knew she did not know him.

A voice. A name called. Her name. "Nakushi! Over here!"

She turned toward the sound of it, and renewed more aches. A woman was approaching, and beside him a young man with a canvas bag dangling from his shoulder by a strap. In his left hand he carried a camera.

The woman waved. "Nakushi." She wobbled her way over the water-worn rocks and finally reached her. Stepping carefully, balanced to protect his camera, the young man drew up alongside the woman.

"Don't you recognize me?" she asked.

In that instant, Nakushi did. "Atasi!" she cried. The women embraced for a moment, before Nakushi drew back. "But... but where are we?"

"This is Bhopal," answered the cameraman. Naveen, Nakushi remembered now, was his name.

"The question is more of when," said Atasi Patel. She handed Nakushi a copy of *The Times of India*. "I bought this a few minutes ago. Look at the date."

Nakushi gasped, and read it aloud. "December 1, 1984." She looked up. "How is that possible?"

Atasi drew a deep breath. "We were hoping you would know."

That stumped Nakushi. "How...how would I know?"

"Because you're..." Atasi stared hard at her. "You mean you don't remember who you are?"

"Of course I do," Nakushi replied, peeved now. "I'm Nakushi Kulasingam. I was born in—"

Atasi's hands fluttered, stopping her. "We know all that. Born in Bombay, lived on the streets, and so forth." A hint of compassion filled her eyes. "You truly do not remember who you are. Oh, Nakushi."

Nakushi spoke through clenched jaws. "Who. Am. I?"

Helpless, Atasi rolled her eyes. "Just say *ashmita*."

"Why would I want to say that?"

"Nakushi," sighed Atasi.

"Oh, very well. *Ashmita!*"

The transformation into Bombay Sapphire was immediate. It shook Atasi and Naveen, and startled the fisherman, who tumbled into the water and rose, dripping, sputtering. It utterly shocked Nakushi, who was swiftly flooded with memories of all the things she had done recently. But not recently; over twenty years ago.

Despite her powers now and her blue tights, she wanted to sit down and think. A flat rock invited her.

"I'm sorry," said Atasi, seating herself alongside. "Realization looked like it hurt you."

"Hurt? No." Bombay Sapphire closed her eyes and allowed herself a few tranquil breaths. "But I do feel like I was hit on the head."

"Do you know why we're here?" she asked. "And why we're here *now*?"

Bombay Sapphire shook her head. "Not yet. But Agni always has a reason for the tasks he gives me. Oh, Atasi! Over twenty years. My sister Savitra…"

"I may be able to call my father and find out." A look of dismay came over her. "Oh, no," she cried. "He may be dead by now."

"We can't think about that, not now," said Bombay Sapphire. "We are here for a reason. Afterwards, if matters are to be made right, Agni will make them so."

"The leak at the plant here in Bhopal," said Atasi. "Over twenty years ago there was a leak. Things died. People, plants. It was serious, but not serious enough. I feel nothing was done to prevent another leak, one that would be far worse."

Bombay Sapphire nodded. Her memory was clearing. She and her two companions had been affected, perhaps killed, by that leak decades ago. Now Agni had sent them ahead in time, to this point in time and space. To do...what?

"I don't know how we can prevent it," she said. "They refused to listen to us before. They would not even allow us to enter the plant. It produces pesticides. One of the chemicals involved is methyl isocyanate. It is highly toxic."

Atasi smiled. "You're definitely Bombay Sapphire," she said. "Nakushi would know nothing of such chemicals."

"She does now. Atasi, I do not feel hunger, but I know you do. Did you see a place nearby where we might find something to eat and drink?"

"After you change back, I think."

"Yes, of course."

* * *

A simple meal of rice and vegetables was followed by a ride in a taxi whose driver was well aware that his passengers came from out of town, and took them the long way around to the pesticide plant in the northern part of the city. Atasi Patel had no idea whether she was still on an expense account for *The Times of India*, but paid the padded fare after the driver dropped them off near where the gas leak had killed them all those years ago. The plants in the vicinity—trees, shrubs, grasses, flowers—still appeared stressed, even more so, and many were moribund. The dwellings in the area had not been improved over the years, but Nakushi had the impression that more of them had been packed closer together. Half-naked children played, darted, and shouted, and the breeze carried the aroma of cooked rice. Toward the south, Nakushi noticed. The same direction the leaked gases would be carried.

They approached as close as they dared. In their attire they stood out both in social class and in purpose. The guards in the shack fifty meters away kept an eye on them, but as long as the three drew no closer and made no overt moves in regard to the plant, there was little the guards could do about it. Still, at any moment, Nakushi expected the police to arrive with questions.

"Over here," she beckoned, and led Atasi and Naveen to the shade of a young banyan tree. There, uncertain, they sat on low rocks. Scraps of wrappers and cigarette stubs at their feet said that others had sat here over the years.

Atasi broke the silence. "I don't see what we can do here, Nakushi," she said, thinking her way. "We can't shut down the plant. Bombay Sapphire could find the leak and close it, perhaps, but what if there is more than one leak? The damage has been building up for years, and the procedures have been ineffective or misdirected." For a moment she considered her words. "And it doesn't matter whether people die as a result of the plant's poor management and maintenance," she added bitterly. "This is India. By now we must have half a billion people. Even the loss of a city is insignificant."

Nakushi glanced around to see if anyone was curious about them. In the shade of the banyan, and among its many tendrils of trunks, they were almost invisible. "*Ashmita*," she said, and transformed.

Atasi gave her a hard yet curious look.

"As you pointed out," said Bombay Sapphire, "I know much more when I am blue. Atasi...I'm not so sure we are here to stop the leaks. I think what will happen is going to happen. Instead, we have been sent here to take measures."

"What measures?" asked Naveen. "What *can* we do?"

"Yes," Bombay Sapphire agreed. "That is by far the better question. It is positive. What *can* we do? We focus on that, not on what we cannot do. But we must act fast, I think. We were not sent here to wait long. How much money do we have among us? Naku...we are carrying about four hundred rupees. Atasi? Naveen?"

"A little over seven hundred," Atasi replied. "But what good—?"

"The gods will always give us the means to do what they want us to do," said Bombay Sapphire. "Otherwise, what would be the point?"

"And how do you know that?" asked Naveen.

"Look at your currency," she told him.

He withdrew a thin wad of bills and opened them up. His face brightened with amazement. "Why...this is this year's money." He riffled through them. "All of them. A thousand rupees."

"But what shall we do with them?" asked Atasi.

"As Nakushi..." At the pronunciation of her name, Bombay Sapphire reverted to her human self. "You and I can do very little, Atasi," she went on. "As Bombay Sapphire, I shouldn't reveal myself just yet. It is Naveen who is best able to do what must be done."

Naveen gaped at her. "And that is?"

"Hire a lorry."

"Why am I—"

"Because they probably will not let a woman hire one," said Nakushi.

"A lorry."

She and Atasi handed him their money. "As large as possible," Nakushi told him. "As quickly as possible. We'll wait right here."

Naveen, after casting her a dubious look, hastened off toward the main part of Bhopal. In the shade of the banyan it was still hot, but the breeze from the north had grown a little stronger. Nakushi and Atasi sat on roots and leaned back against the boles.

"I'm not sure what you have in mind," said Atasi.

"The only thing we can do," said Nakushi. "The leak is going to happen, and I think very soon. Perhaps even tonight or tomorrow. We can't stop it. What we can do is evacuate as many people as possible. We'll take them to Gora, near the very south shore of the lake. They should be safe there, and there will be people to help."

Atasi made an irritated sound. "And what will we tell them, Nakushi? Get in the truck or else? Many won't go."

"But some will." She spread her hands in a helpless gesture. "We have to try, Atasi. We have to save as many as we can."

Atasi was still not convinced. "Driving through Bhopal to get there? We could make two, maybe three trips."

"Not driving," said Nakushi, and grinned. "Flying."

"Oh. Oh! Well, of course."

"We do what we can, as is expected of us." She leaned back and closed her eyes. "You should get some rest. You're going to need it."

003

The air hovering over Mount Meru trembled, though the voices were not raised. Lord Shiva was well-aware that anger was counter-productive. Still, what the god of storms had done was tantamount to interference in the plans of a superior god.

And Agni was unapologetic, even though three of Shiva's arms now wielded scimitars. "Bombay Sapphire is interspersed among human events," he argued. "Though not a goddess, she nevertheless is revered throughout history. She gives hope where there is no justice. She is rich with help in a land that is crushingly poor. She works the will of a god, which is to say myself; that counts as my own actions count. I did not realize," he added, with a bit of a bite, "that you had already established the death toll you desired. There will be little room on the *samsara* this day."

"Surely you can appreciate the side effects," Shiva countered. Two of his scimitars swished through the air, bestirring a breeze that spilled down the side of a mountain and ruptured roofing in the hamlet below. "The government of Bharat," he used the true name of India, "will be compelled to supervise the corporate colonialists more closely."

"As if you cared for that," spat Agni.

"I care nothing for that," Shiva replied calmly. "It is you who cares for it. Yet you will not thank me." A pregnant pause followed. "You must withdraw her and her allies."

"I will do no such thing," Agni shot back. His voice now raised a thunderstorm over the Ganges. "People expect her to act, even though there is little that she can do. Lord Shiva, please be reasonable. She will save a few hundred, perhaps a thousand. You will have your thousands of deaths. Let it be as it will."

A scimitar vanished. "You will do well not to interfere with me again, O Agni of Storms," warned Shiva, and vanished as well.

*　　*　　*

It took over an hour for Naveen to return with the lorry. An old blue truck with white detailing, it had seen far better days. The engine sounded rough, and the trickle of smoke from the exhaust pipe suggested that it was burning a bit of oil. Still it ran, and Naveen parked it to one side of the road leading up to the guard shack, shut off the engine, and got out, while Nakushi and Atasi inspected the vehicle. Properly stuffed, it might hold as many as twenty people inside. Nakushi was more concerned with the lorry's rust. As Bombay Sapphire, she meant to fly the vehicle to safety; she did not want passengers falling from the sky through the flimsy siding. Here and there she kicked the walls and siding; it seemed strong enough. But for how many flights? That was something she could not control.

"I think we have to start now," said Nakushi. "We'll each take a section of housing, and tell them the truth: there's a leak in the pesticide plant and we have to evacuate. Do not waste time trying to persuade people to leave. We'll save as many as we can. That's all we can do."

Nakushi met with failure at the first hut she tried. The woman inside was only in her forties, but already wrinkled, her skin dried from proximity to the faint but ever-present fumes in the vicinity. Seven children of various ages, the younger ones naked, milled around inside, looking bored. Some of them had runny noses. Nakushi spoke simply and clearly, and had not completed half of what she wanted to say when the woman simply closed the door.

Nakushi resisted the impulse to shift to the blue and force the evacuation. As far as she could see, that would only make things worse, and without a guard at the lorry the woman and her children would flee the first chance they got.

She moved to the next house, occupied by another woman of the same age and her teenage son. No one else was at home. Here she gained an ear, and after only a couple of questions, they gathered up a few belongings and accompanied her to the lorry.

"I've always known there was something wrong here," said the woman, her voice cracked and dry. "I told our council, and they took notes, but nothing was ever done."

"Just wait here until we have a full load," said Nakushi. "And please don't be afraid. We'll get you away from here."

Both Naveen and Atasi arrived with small families. Nakushi kept count, and decided that another four or so would fit inside. Atasi moved off to see to this, while Nakushi again looked over the undercarriage for the best spot to lift the lorry. Nowhere looked particularly good, but with Agni's help she believed she would succeed. When Atasi returned with a family of three, Nakushi transformed, and hoped for the best.

In the truck, someone cried out and pointed at her. But there was no fright in her voice, only amazement. "I thought she was a legend," she cried out. "The gods are with us! It's her! It's Bombay Sapphire!"

Bombay Sapphire wondered whether her face turned red or darker blue with the blush that surged up through her.

"We're going to fly," she told them. "Hold on, and stay inside until we land."

And with that, they were off.

Dusk approached. The lorry had survived twenty-two loads. Already a couple of pieces had fallen off while Bombay Sapphire had the vehicle in flight. One was the rear bumper, loosened in a collision years ago. By the time she returned, Atasi and Naveen had gathered another sixteen people, including nine children. The passengers looked frightened and uncertain. Atasi and Naveen looked harried and exhausted.

"We have to keep going," urged Bombay Sapphire. "We can sleep later."

"Just a short break," pleaded Atasi, breathing heavily.

Bombay Sapphire gazed up at the sky. She expected no answers or solutions from that quarter, but perhaps Agni was watching. No words of his came to her.

"All right, let's get them loaded up," she said. "I'll take them south, while you two sit down for a while. When I get back, I'll transform and help you gather more—"

"Nakushi," cried Atasi, her arm shaking as she pointed.

Two blocks away, people were falling down. Whatever was killing them was immediately fatal.

"Get in the lorry," yelled Bombay Sapphire. "Don't look back."

One more time, please, she thought, sliding under the vehicle to grasp the rusted undercarriage. More people fell; the gas was drifting closer. She pushed up, and the front axle cracked and broke. Inside the lorry, people screamed. The sounds and the fear galvanized her. She had no choice; the lorry had to hold together one more time. Once more she pushed, and rose into the air.

Bombay Sapphire kept to a low altitude, just above the roofs and the light poles. Metal creaked above her. She had horrible visions of the lorry splitting open like an egg, spilling its terrified contents onto houses, pavement, other vehicles. There was only so much she could do. Agni, she thought. "Agni," she called out. But there was no response. Or no audio response. The lorry, however, seemed to be holding together.

She flew on.

All those people. How many would it kill? Thousands? One breath, and it was over. Methyl isocyanate. Instant death. It worked on insects. It worked on people. She knew what the corporate attitude was: India had hundreds of millions of people. Considering the profits being gained at the plant, surely a few thousand deaths would hardly matter. Anger made her growl. But she had not been sent by Agni for her rage and outrage. She had been sent to save lives, as many as she could. Over four hundred people would live to see another day. It wasn't enough. But it was all she would get.

She was crying when she touched down with the lorry. Even as its tires reached the ground, the vehicle began to fall apart. A fender fell, another bent out. Metallic creaks and groans wrought the air as passengers stumbled free, and were helped by those already rescued. Bombay Sapphire moved off a little way by herself, stricken now with grief, allowing herself to fully feel, now that she had done all she could. Trembling shook her to her core. She herself had been in no danger, but that fact had eluded her time after time, with each rescuing flight of the lorry. Death seemed to yap incessantly at her heels. She and her companions had worked a miracle.

But why were all the deaths necessary? It was not a question she could ask Agni. One did not question the wishes of gods and goddesses. They were a force of nature...just as she had become a force of nature, for she was the *asura* created and designated by Agni. She was, in effect, his avatar on Earth. But she could not fight death; she could but aid the living.

Onto the grass she spilled now. A distant part of her wondered how she, with all her powers, could feel exhaustion. Was it merely in her mind, derived by the sum of her efforts even though she did not feel those efforts physically? There was so much, despite those powers, that she did not understand.

Helplessness wearied her soul. For a moment, she thought to hear screaming, but the toxic gas killed instantly, stopping the screams stillborn. Perhaps it came from the echoes of dead souls.

Presently she stopped wondering. She had done all she could. It would have to be enough. She closed her eyes, as if it were for the last time...

004

Once more, Bombay Sapphire awoke on a cloud. The sense of time escaped her. She might have just arrived; she might have lain here since Brahman took the first handfuls of his substance and cast it to form Creation. The air carried a light chill, and she hugged herself as proof against it. A girl arrived before her, floating down from somewhere unseen, dressed in lavender gossamer, dark eyes outlined in *kohl*; carrying prepared fruit and clots of curried rice and vegetables on a silver tray. Bombay Sapphire thought the girl might be the same one who had served her earlier; *apsaras*, even budding ones, were difficult to distinguish from one another. She did not speak, but displayed her wares to Bombay Sapphire, who gratefully took the tray from her. Hunger did not abate on Mount Meru.

Sparingly, while the girl waited, she ate the rice and vegetables, and finished with a few bits of melon. Finished, she made a little gesture, and the girl took the tray and simply faded away. The food did nothing to slake the emptiness inside her. Questions began to form, but there was no one to whom to address them. All in good time, she thought, in a place where time did not exist. Presently she assumed the lotus position, three-finger mudhras resting on her thighs, eyes gently closed to wait for all time.

When Bombay Sapphire opened her eyes again, she was no longer alone. Beside her, also in lotus, sat the girl who had served her—or one very much like her. But it was the other two figures who required her attention. Lightning Bearer and Six Arms had returned, garbed in gowns of red, yellow, and ochre, and carrying the symbols of their godhood.

Six Arms spoke first, and to her, but grudgingly, even though his left middle arm held a curved sword in the position of a salute. "You have done well." He did not have to add, "For an *asura*."

Bombay Sapphire ignored him. "What is thy bidding, O Agni?"

"That is...under discussion," Lightning Bearer told her.

"May I ask, O Agni?" A tiny gesture bade her continue. "How many died...?"

Lightning Bearer looked to Six Arms for the response. "Thirty-seven thousand," he said. "The count continues. It should clear forty thousand."

"And this pleases you?" gasped Bombay Sapphire.

Before Six Arms could retort, Lightning Bearer stepped in front of him. Holding a clutch of lightning bolts, he said, "I put it to you succinctly: there are but four possibilities. She returns to the time she just came from. She remains here. She ascends. She returns to her own time."

"There is a fifth alternative," growled Six Arms. "She is your creation. Decreate her, and let her proceed to the *samsara*."

"I had not finished," Lightning Bearer said stiffly. "She has two companions. They are to share her fate."

"Brahma did not decree this."

"You are correct," replied Lightning Bearer. "It is I who have said it."

"Then let us see what Brahma and Vishnu have to say."

A burst of white light accompanied their disappearance. As it faded, Bombay Sapphire found herself alone with the fledgling *apsara*, again to wait for all time.

"Can you speak?" she asked the girl.

After a quick and furtive look around, the girl shook her head.

Bombay Sapphire considered this. "Are you enjoined from speaking to me?"

This time, after another check of her surroundings, she nodded, just once.

Bombay Sapphire studied the remains of the meal on the tray. "Thank you for this," she blurted.

"You are wel—" Both the girl's hands covered her mouth, and fearful eyes outlined in *kohl* now swept frantically from side to side.

Bombay Sapphire said gently, "It is my wish that you speak with me. If there is fault, it is mine. If Brahma and Vishnu should decide in my favor, you will be forgiven. If not, you shall join me on the *samsara*."

"You...you have much privilege."

"I am but a servant of Agni." Briefly she regarded the *apsara*-in-training. "How are you called?"

"I-I have no name."

"Then your name shall be Daalachini, and I shall think of you always as Daala."

Solemnly the girl inclined her head in acknowledgement. In the next moment, darkness swallowed Bombay Sapphire.

*   *   *

Atasi Patel sat in her office at *The Times of India*, blinking. Something had just happened, she was certain of that, but she had no idea what it might have been. At the open doorway, leaning against the jamb, stood Naveen, the photographer and recorder assigned to her. He, too, seemed to look as if he had suddenly and unexpectedly materialized out of thin air. Even his whites —shirt and trousers—looked as if they had just come from the cleaners.

"You'd better sit down," Atasi told him. "Before you fall down. Did you have a late night?"

He grinned sheepishly as he obeyed. "That is what it feels like. But if I did, it would be nice to be able to remember it."

"What have you got for me?"

He looked at the camera as if he had never seen it before. "I-I don't know. I have this memory of taking photographs, but of what, and of where I was..." He left off with a shrug.

"Then hadn't you better develop the film and find out what's on them?"

Naveen stood back up. His voice sounded more stable now. "Yes. Yes, of course."

After he left, Atasi leaned back in her chair and stretched her legs. She noted with some alacrity that she was wearing Western blue jeans and tennis shoes along with her more traditional white blouse. The outfit felt more comfortable, and was more practical, than a sari. Even so, her attire was, she knew, the object of comments and not a little derision from the male journalists and staff. I am the future, she told herself, as she had often told them. Get used to it.

Presently she shut her eyes. A few meditative breaths cleared her mind, and left space for ideas and memories to filter back in. What she wanted was the return of whatever project she had been working on only moments earlier. What she saw, what gradually filtered into her mind, was a factory of some sort, with pipes and towers and a great block structure beside a smaller one, evidently an office of some sort. But when had she been working on that? Whatever it was?

She opened her eyes, and dismissed the vision. What else, what else? Some scraps of notepaper on her desk invited examination. She leafed through them;

nothing suggested itself save the note for her to pick up rice and Gupta sodas on the way home. When had she written that?

Irwin Cross, the correspondent from the BBC and a resident of Bombay since World War II, stopped by to lean against the doorjamb. "Are you feeling all right?" he asked her. His shock of pale gray hair looked as if he had been playing with a Van de Graaff generator. But his suit was Saville Row—not a reference she understood, but assumed it to mean that it had cost him some money, even if the gray trousers and lemon jacket did not blend all that well. Despite his fifty years in this climate, his deeply tanned face had few wrinkles, but these seemed to deepen as he regarded her.

The inquiry puzzled her. "Why do you ask?"

"You look...pale. Perhaps you should drink some water."

She nodded. "Perhaps you're right."

"Take care of yourself," he admonished. "You're a good journalist. We need you."

The compliment made her beam as she watched him stroll away down the hall. Before she could recover her thoughts, Naveen returned, with an expression as grave as she had ever seen on him. He thrust several photographs onto her desk, and flopped down in the chair reserved for visitors. His breathing sounded rapid and shallow.

Atasi fingered the photographs to her, and studied each one in turn. One was almost an exact replica of the structure she had seen during her meditation. It made her gasp. But what was it?

"Your expression," breathed Naveen. "You've seen this place as well."

She nodded slowly. "But I don't recall…"

He sat up straight. "That's just it. Neither do I!"

"I-I don't understand…"

"Exactly." He tilted his head to one side, thinking. "Would your friend Nakushi know it?"

"As Bombay Sapphire, you mean…oh, wait! I think she was there, too!"

"But where is *there*?"

Again she pored over the photographs. About to nudge the third one away, she abruptly slid it back. "There's a lorry," she cried, jabbing a fingertip at it. "Just there. It says—I can just make out some letters on the siding—'bho…" She looked up at him. "Bhopal?"

Naveen looked as if his heart were fluttering. "But I have never been to Bhopal. I've only been in Madhya Pradesh two, three times, but never there."

Atasi got to her feet. "I think I had better go find Nakushi," she said. "Bring your camera." She scooped up the photographs. "I'll bring these."

005

Nakushi came to on a platform in a banyan tree that overlooked a courtyard and a shrine of freshly-quarried pink stone. Through dense overhead foliage, sunlight filtered down on her, warming her as she lay sprawled on the hard wood. Blinking helped to clear her vision and bring her surroundings into focus. Someone was sitting nearby on the platform: a boy, perhaps eleven years old, attired in white short pants that seemed to glisten even in the shadows where he sat. He was chewing on a bite of fruit—a mango, she thought.

His name came to her: Agneya. With the name came the associated memories. He had been an associate and yes, even advisor, to Bombay Sapphire since the time of her empowerment by Agni.

I'm home, she thought, and sat up to dangle her lower legs over the edge of the platform. Ten meters below ran a dirt road that turned to mud and mire during the monsoons. She flashed the boy a wry smile.

"Does Manish know you're filching his fresh fruit?" she asked him.

Manish was the Vedic priest in charge of the shrine to Agni. She glanced over the courtyard, but he was nowhere in sight.

Agneya thrust the half-eaten mango at her. "Would you like a bite?"

Still she smiled. "And now you wish to make me an accomplice?"

He laughed, as she had known he would. But he quickly sobered. "What do you remember?"

In a flash she saw everything that had transpired in the Bhopal of the future. Her head ached. She clapped her hands to her ears and rocked back and forth, eyes squeezed shut, as if to block the images. Instead, she trapped them inside her. She fell back to the hard wood, faint, fainting.

* * *

"She's alive?" gasped Savitra. "You told me she was dead. You promised me!"

"The gods are in control of your sister's fate," said Kallia. The black demon sat back in the stuffed armchair and crossed her tights-clad legs, relishing the moment. Off-balance, Savitra was easier to control. "I do as they say," Kallia went on. "As you do. They need not explain themselves to such as us."

"Yes, yes, of course," said Savitra. She plucked at silken fabric over her shoulder. "As above, so below. It's just that..."

"Nakushi is busy just now," said Kallia. "She will not interfere in our work. Now, then: several people have been recruited to replace those lost to the predations of Bombay Sapphire. It is your duty as leader of the Deccan Dholes to meet with them, to establish in their eyes the chain of command. I have set the meeting for two o'clock this afternoon." She eyed Savitra with her usual disdain. "You will wear your white office suit," she ordered. "And not a sari."

"Very well," Savitra said stiffly. "Is there anything else?"

The black demon made a dismissive gesture. As she did so, she read Savitra's thoughts. *Someday*, the girl hissed darkly. *Someday*. Kallia smiled to herself. If Savitra was determined to get some of her own back, that might be useful to exploit.

* * *

When Nakushi awoke again, the images had passed, and with them much of the memories they represented. Agneya said softly, "Go to the shrine entrance. You are about to have visitors."

The fabric of her tangerine and lemon sari snagged on a few branches as she climbed down from the tree. Freeing herself, she made her way around the pink stone wall to the opening that led into the courtyard. Around her people made their way thither and yon over the dirt pathways of the great slum of Dharavi. Several of them, recognizing her, either smiled or made a little gesture of acknowledgement, but did not slow for her as they passed. Although she was of their caste, she carried an additional weight on her shoulders, for her name, Nakushi, meant unwanted. But as

Bombay Sapphire, she was needed. That was enough.

As she reached the entranceway, a red Hillman Minx that had seen better days pulled up to the kerb nearby and parked. Atasi Patel and Naveen emerged from it, but instead of crossing the street to meet her, they beckoned, and turned toward a tea kiosk, there to await her. By the time she reached them, they had already ordered black tea for her, without the stick of cinnamon that was customarily included to stir the tea. As Nakushi accepted the cup gratefully, she noted that neither Atasi nor Naveen had sticks; even a whiff of cinnamon could make her pass out.

"You remembered," said Nakushi, sipping tentatively at her cup.

Atasi gave her a serious look. "But what do *you* remember?" she asked.

"Flying," she replied. "Lifting. People running, screaming, falling..."

"In Bhopal?" asked Naveen.

Nakushi nodded. "I think so. It's all so vague, and growing dimmer even as we speak." She made a face, frustrated. "I'm sorry. I'm not much help. But I cannot escape the feeling that the three of us did something good."

"I feel that as well," said Atasi, nodding. She showed Nakushi the photographs that had come from Naveen's camera.

One by one Nakushi looked them over. Each was a spark that illuminated a brief flash of memory. She was on the verge of suggesting that the three of them go to Bhopal to investigate when a vision struck her, blinding her momentarily. Swaying, she leaned against the side of the kiosk, and shut her eyes.

"Nakushi?" worried Atasi.

For long moments she did not respond. Her eyelids rose to reveal eyes scrolled up so far that only white showed. Back and forth she rocked, in tempo to some sounds only she could hear. The few sounds she emitted were those of animals: barking, a sonorous growl, a bird call, all so soft that only Atasi and Naveen could hear. Within a moment these faded, and she slumped against Atasi.

Presently Nakushi's eyes returned to normal. Only then did she realize that she had spilled her tea all over herself and the sidewalk. Ruefully she plucked at her sari, but her words were directed elsewhere.

"I must go to Burhanpur," she said. "You are to return to Bhopal and—"

"But we have not been there," Naveen protested.

Nakushi described the vision she had just experienced. "Have you looked at your notebook today?" she asked Atasi.

"Well...no." She removed it from her purse and leafed through it. Toward the end of the notes she stared wide-eyed. "When did I write this?" she asked, and glanced at Naveen. "These seem to match some of the photographs you found in your camera."

"Try to find out as much as you can about maintenance in the pesticide plant," said Nakushi. "Write an exposé and support it with the photographs. Make it sound...I don't know. Ominous? A leak there could kill tens of thousands. Use the exposé to draw attention to this. But be very careful there; Union Carbide will not cooperate with you."

"Where are you going?" asked Naveen.

Nakushi smiled mysteriously. "I have to change clothes," she said, still plucking at the silk. "After that, I go to the Yawal Sanctuary."

With that, she turned away and went back across the street to the temple entrance. After checking inside to see that the courtyard was unoccupied, she stepped into the shadows and uttered a single word.

"*Ashmita.*"

* * *

The flight to the border between the states of Maharashtra and Madhya Pradesh required a minor detour for Bombay Sapphire, to prevent herself from being spotted by the pilot of an airliner on its way south. Startling him might lead to a crash. In any event, she would have had to bear east eventually, for that was where the Sanctuary lay, in some highlands to the west of Burhanpur. For once, Agni had been very specific about what he wanted from her. This was not a simple task like going to Arunachal Pradesh to drop huge boulders on invading Chinese tanks. No, he had given her a thorough briefing.

Yawal Wildlife Sanctuary had been established to protect the area from deforestation and from poachers. Its forests covered the rugged and rolling terrain like a great green blanket, but a blanket that had been "torn" here and there by the uncontrolled harvesting of trees. Over the past several years the damage had lessened, as the Sanctuary staff began to take more direct action, with guidance and authority from New Delhi. But a new wave of infiltrators had arrived, coming not for trees, but for tigers.

Her visit to the Sanctuary was hardly official. With no reason to stop and declare herself, she overflew the headquarters and staff residences and looked for a small clearing in which to land and gather her purposes. With the dangers not only from the animals but also from the poachers and the lumber harvesters, she decided to remain as Bombay Sapphire. As she touched down, monkeys announced their objections to her arrival. She smiled up at them, and one or two shied nuts down at her. She estimated her distance from the buildings at five miles. The time had come to listen to the sounds of the tropical forest.

In places the foliage was so dense that she could scarcely peer into it. What she was searching for was clothing that stood out against the green, and slight movement against the direction of whatever breezes flowed within. Arboreal wildlife was also an indicator. Although the monkeys had given her a raucous greeting, she suspected that the forests would grow silent if there were poachers lurking about. She began to creep into the woods. She had no fear of snakes—cobras and kraits, mostly—and even the great rock pythons were unable to damage her, although she did not look forward to untangling herself from their coils. All the while she moved, she listened and looked. But there was nothing amiss, as far as she could tell.

Thick fronds moist with dew and condensation brushed against her skin. The water beaded and trickled away; it could not dampen her, but it did lend a small measure of relief from the oppressive heat and humidity. From time to time she paused, to listen and to look. A city dweller by history, she felt out of place in the wild like this. Yet Agni had sent her; she could but obey.

A leaf shook overhead, showering her. A bird had taken flight, silently. Just as silently, she apologized. She had been sent here to protect, not to frighten. Very still she stood now, as if in anticipation of some tropical event. Watchful, wary, she scarcely blinked. Yes, there it was, on the bole of a tree: a snake, green and brown, blending with the bark itself. It seemed poised, not as if to strike, but in expectation of the arrival of a meal. She took a step, and it turned a spatulate head toward her. She froze, and after a moment it looked away again.

The jungle, she decided, would take some getting used to.

The report of a firearm shattered the mood around her. It came from somewhere north of her, impossible to pinpoint with any precision. She rose into the air, fifty meters above the canopy, and flew off in that direction. Below her the foliage was impenetrable, but she was coming upon a clearing. Cautiously she approached—not from fear of being shot at, but of scaring away her quarry—and finally hovered, lowering herself to the top of the canopy.

There. Two men, in jungle fatigues and caps, and armed with rifles. But there was no victim. Whatever they had fired at, they had missed. Likely, she concluded, it was a tiger, stealthy against the branches and grass and bamboo. It was even possible that the men had fired at shadows. If a tiger were charging, they would have one shot before it reached them. They would have fired at any movement.

Without further reflection, Bombay Sapphire swooped down to the jungle floor, her fists struck the men in the back, just below the nape of the neck. In the same flight, she caught up the limp men and flew them north, over Madhya Pradesh. There while they were still unconscious, she hovered two miles in the air and considered.

It was not in her to kill the two men except in defense of a victim, despite serious temptation. But Agni had left the disposal of poachers in her hands by virtue of his having issued no specific instructions. What, then was a suitable punishment? Presently she looked north, at the distant Himalayas.

Half an hour later, the men began to struggle and scream. Harsh instructions followed from her: continue to struggle, and I shall drop you. Wide-eyed as they looked down, the pair relented. Another hour later, still paralyzed by terror, they looked down at the soaring snowcapped mountains of southern Himachal Pradesh state and the city of Shimla. There, before a small Buddhist temple—she could not leave the men to the cold and the elements—she gave them her final orders.

"If you go to Yawal Sanctuary again, you will find this punishment to be as nothing, compared to what I will do to you then."

Without awaiting their response, she flew straight up three miles, and then away to the south.

* * *

When night fell in the Yawal Sanctuary, it landed hard. Starlight failed to penetrate the canopy, and there was no moon. Yet there was vision. The nocturnal denizens of the tropical forest were able to see well enough to capture prey and to avoid becoming prey. Within a minute, Bombay Sapphire could see her surroundings as clearly as if it were day. But there were no poachers afoot. They would wait until dawn. So would she.

Still, she walked, and sometimes she flew at a low height, swishing through fronds and branches. Here and there, small animals skittered. Bioluminescent insects made themselves known. But there were no people.

As she lowered herself to the ground once more, a great maw clamped onto her left ankle. Links of a chain rang out. Overhead, monkeys squawked and birds fluttered. A larger animal, possibly a deer, blundered between the trees. Bombay Sapphire felt no pain as she sat down on the forest floor and opened the steel trap. Her fingers ran over the teeth, and found many of them bent or blunted by striking her leg. Leaving the trap closed and harmless, she stood up and very still, listening to the night. It seemed unlikely that poachers were active; they would stop by in the morning to see what, if anything, they had caught.

She climbed up into a great tree, found a suitable branch, and went to sleep.

006

In Bhopal, Atasi Patel and Naveen took adjoining rooms in a simple hotel within walking distance of the Union Carbide pesticide plant. In the morning they met in the hotel restaurant for breakfast, none the worse for having slept on inexpensive mattresses and pillows. Atasi's jet hair was still slightly damp from her shower, and left darker marks around the collar of her gray blouse. She tried a roll from the little platter and found it palatable.

"Now what?" asked Naveen, grinning.

"It will be mostly your work, I'm afraid," she told him. She knew he understood, although the subject had never been broached between them: a man could receive cooperation far more readily than a woman. "And I'm not sure what to ask for. I was hoping you might know."

His grin faded only a little. "That sounds ominous."

She shook her head. "I don't think it is. What I want are clean containers, the size of a small jar, that can be sealed tightly. Ten of them, let's say. Probably glass jars would do, but it's the tightness of the seal that is important. I thought an apothecary might have something of the kind."

"I think I'm already ahead of you," he said.

She smiled. "I think you are."

"Let me see if I can guess the rest," he said, trying a roll. "Sometime after midnight, when all is dark and the guard is trying without success not to doze off, you want me to take air samples from around the plant."

"That is a good guess," she acknowledged. "But it is not so simple. Five random spots, each a good distance from the others, with samples taken at ground level and at...nose level. You'd better get some sticky labels, too."

"And you? What will you be doing?"

"I'll be in Public Records, trying to get copies of the layout of the plant, as well as the building permits, any requests for exceptions..."

Naveen frowned. "Such as?"

"I won't know until I look," she replied. "I was thinking maybe they wanted specific permission to manufacture—or use in the manufacturing process—a substance that might otherwise have been prohibited."

This worried Naveen further. "You may be looking at money changing hands."

"Probably. And I suspect the clerk will notify Union Carbide of my investigation." She shrugged. "Appa never told me this work would be safe."

"You'd better call him and let him know what you...we, are about to do."

"It's already on my list. Finish your roll."

* * *

The distant sound of some great thrashing beast in distress awoke Bombay Sapphire just after dawn. She sensed pain, and rubbed her left ankle as she descended from the tree. Tilting her head this way and that, she soon determined that the sound was coming from the west, further into the Sanctuary. With steady caution—she had no wish to disturb the jungle denizens unnecessarily—she made her way through the tropic forest, noting only that the sounds were growing louder as she approached, and that she now heard some grunting of effort as well.

Into a clearing she burst, and spotted the elephant on the other side of it. It was a young male with meter-long curved tusks, and its left front foot was caught in a metal trap attached to a massive tree by thick chain links. She saw immediately that there was no way the tusker was going to free himself.

She had the power to open those toothed metal jaws around his ankle. But he was going to have to calm himself for her to do it. And she had no idea how to make him understand that she was here to help him.

Approaching slowly, Bombay Sapphire tried humming a tune. It seemed to have little effect, except that she was now certain that he had noticed her, and that as yet he had not reacted in any way to her presence. She hoped that was a good sign, but as she drew near, he swung his trunk at her. The tip of it grazed her shoulder, and she withdrew a little. He resumed his struggles with the trap.

She needed help.

Agni might be summoned, but he would expect her to figure out what to do, else why send her here in the first place? She eased back another couple of steps, until she stood against one of the lesser trees that surrounded the clearing. The trapped elephant's efforts did not diminish, but neither did they cause even the tree's leaves to tremble. Already blood was seeping from around the metal teeth. She steeled herself against the sounds of the tusker's anguish.

"Ganesh," she said softly, summoning the god of elephants. "I beg you, please help your creature. If he is calm, I can free him. You know this to be true, and you know my heart. Please help him and me."

Now she stepped forward and raised a hand. The elephant paused in his efforts, as if wondering what she was now about. Gently she placed her hand on his trunk, her body within easy reach of his tusks. He could not harm her, but he would not know that. He merely watched her, and held his trunk still. She slid her hand down the trunk to his shoulder, and from there down to his great leg. Kneeling before him, she grasped the two jaws and easily separated them. Blood continued to flow as he lifted his leg free. She let the jaws slam shut again.

When she rose again, she realized that he had not moved away. Across species their eyes met. She raised her hand again, and placed it once more on his trunk. He wrapped the trunk once around her arm, then pulled back slowly to free her limb.

He turned away and melted into the jungle. She watched him until he was out of sight.

"Thank you, Ganesh," she whispered. "He will be safe now, but please see to his foot." She became aware of aching ribs. Suddenly she took a breath, and understood that she had not done so for a couple of minutes.

With loathing she looked down at the trap. Those who had emplaced it would sure come to check on it, probably daily. She inspected the chain, and found that it was simply locked around the tree. She released it and dragged the trap to the next tree, securing it there and covering it with leaves and jungle detritus. Then she climbed into the tree to watch and to wait, and to warn away any animals that came near.

After almost an hour, the sunlight that dappled Bombay Sapphire through the foliage began to relax her to the point of drifting off. At the sound of a twig snapping, she started awake to find a solitary man in a camouflage outfit advancing toward the tree where the trap had been hidden. He was a swarthy, dark-skinned man with a week's beard, and Bombay Sapphire thought he might be of southern India origin. With a stick he carefully shed the leaves from around where he expected the trap to be, and found nothing. Nor was any chain visible around the trunk.

Abruptly he straightened, and spun around wildly, as if he expected to see some monster trailing a trap and a length of heavy chain. But there was nothing, nor was there any sound from the jungle. Satisfied that he was still alone, he returned to the task of moving the detritus away from the trap site, to be certain that the trap was gone.

Finished, he looked up, dark eyes filled with questions. What was in his opinion not possible had happened. He began to look around for signs that the trap had been dragged off. At this tree and that he paused for a cursory inspection, but there was nothing to see. Eventually he reached the tree where Bombay Sapphire hovered above him, invisible in the foliage.

He screamed with the next step he took. The trap's cruel jaws caught him just above the ankle. He collapsed onto the grass and leaves, in too much pain to concentrate on opening, if possible, the trap and freeing his leg. Already his camouflage trousers were dark with blood. Again and again he cried out. He tried to kick his leg and succeeded only in tightening the chain. A question caused his cries to wane. He stared at the tree, as if wondering whether he had simply searched the wrong one.

Only then did he notice the tiger that had just emerged into the clearing.

It came to an abrupt stop, tail twitching as its yellow eyes suspiciously surveyed the man. Clearly the presence of edible prey had not been anticipated. Once seen, it was impossible not to turn down. But the tiger very slowly placed one paw before the other, not toward the man but to circle around him, to be certain he presented no threat. He was halfway to the man when Bombay Sapphire dropped out of the trees and landed on the ground some two paces in front of the man, and perhaps ten paces from the tiger.

Startled, the tiger roared, and edged back a couple of steps.

Still in a crouch, Bombay Sapphire watched the predator carefully. It seemed nervous, and if it were afraid, it might well charge instead of retreat. Surely two puny humans posed no real threat to it. But she had dropped down to protect the man. Despite the cruelty of the trap he had set, as with the men before him, she had no wish to kill him, or to see him killed because of the trap she had set for him. She might of course kill the tiger, but that would defeat the very purpose for which she had been sent to the Sanctuary by Agni.

What she had to do, then, was make the tiger go away, so that she could free the man and get him to medical care. All she had to do now was figure out how to make a hungry tiger abandon an easy meal.

As unobtrusively as possible, Bombay Sapphire sat down on the grass in tailor fashion—not in the lotus, for she might have to move quickly—and placed three-finger *mudhras* on her thighs. Her eyes narrowed, so that she could just make out the shape and movements of the great cat. Softly, in a low but steady voice, she began a mantra.

"*Gati gati paragati parasamgati bodhi svaha.*"

This she repeated over and over again, swaying gently back and forth as she did so. Her intent was to lull the tiger, not to sleep, but into thinking that no one else was present in the clearing. Even as she spoke, she did not exist. She was not there. The man, mostly hidden behind her, was not there. After two of her mantras, she whispered to him to be as silent as possible, for only in that way might she save him.

"*Gati gati paragati parasamgati bodhi svaha.*"

Again and again, like the soft call of a bird high in the tree.

The tiger looked in her direction, but its eyes no longer seemed focused. It was not seeing her. It could not see her. The clearing was empty. There was nothing to eat here.

"*Gati gati paragati parasamgati bodhi svaha.*"

The tiger gave one last long look in her direction, as if wondering where the food he had seen earlier had gotten to, and wandered off into the jungle.

Bombay Sapphire continued her soft chanting and rocking for a good five minutes before she brought them to a close. Turning back to the trapped poacher, she opened the trap jaws as if they were cooked noodles, and waited while he extracted his foot. From the appearance of the injury, she concluded that the bones of the lower leg had been cracked. Blood continued to ooze from the teeth punctures. None of this could be helped; he needed medical attention. She lifted him in her arms, told him to relax, and flew off to the north.

007

Two hours later, Bombay Sapphire and the poacher arrived at the small town of Kamet at the foot of the great Himalayas. There she sought out the clinic where Neelam Halder was the sole physician, and carried the poacher into the examination room, rather to the surprise of Maryam, the chief nurse.

Almost immediately, Halder arrived. Ever professional, he began to examine the poacher, meanwhile casting glances every so often in Bombay Sapphire's direction. She in turn remembered her previous visit, which she had brought refugees from a landslide to his clinic. Especially she recalled the night that had transpired afterwards.

Not quite thirty, Halder was her height, and she was able to gaze evenly into his eyes. He had the lighter brown skin often found in northwestern India, and a Hindi accent when he spoke English. In his presence, she had transformed to Nakushi in order to provide blood for a patient's transfusion. She had told him of her name, but not of the sordid past that went with it. A past he had dismissed out of hand, for she had had to survive. For him, only the present had signified. And in that present, she had been with him.

Now, Bombay Sapphire smiled to herself, remembering, and wondering how much of their relationship had been the intent of Agni, who had dispatched her to save the refugees.

Finally, the initial examination completed, Halder sent the poacher off with the nurse for X-rays and other treatment. He sat down beside Bombay Sapphire on the bench; they did not quite touch.

"What is his background?" he asked her, still professional.

"He was an ivory poacher in Yawal Wildlife Sanctuary," she explained simply. "He had set a trap for an elephant, but I caught him in his trap."

"Agni sent you there, did he?"

A faint smile curled the corners of her mouth. "So well you know me."

"I have hoped you would return, Nakushi," he said quietly, looking at his hands in his lap. "I have missed you."

"Do you wish me to transform?"

"Unless you know how to get those blue tights off you."

Her burst of laughter was a glorious thing, filling the examination room and reverberating throughout it. She turned him to her and threw her arms around him, still laughing. Her, "Nakushi," made her transform while she was still in his arms.

In the early evening, the duty day finished, Nakushi and Halder were sitting outside the clinic on the wooden bench just away from the drip line of a large mango tree, where they had sat a couple months ago after treating the refugees. Once again, the stars above them bled their feeble light. Across the way, electric light through a window was just bright enough to cast shadows. They continued to sit not quite touching, as if physical contact would have proved too much for them to bear. Nakushi felt herself trembling. There was a quiver in her voice when she spoke.

"In the morning," she said, "I shall have to return to Yawal Sanctuary."

"In the morning," he repeated, hopefully.

"I do not believe Agni will begrudge me this time with you, Neelam. If there were some urgency to my return, he would already have advised me of it."

"I have some rice and vegetable curry, if you are hungry," he said.

"I am not hungry," she said carefully, "for food."

In the early morning Nakushi awoke in a tangle of quilt and sheet to find Neelam Halder lying on his left side, head supported on hand and elbow as he quietly regarded her. She realized she had awakened at least partially by the sense that she was being watched over. He gave her a few moments to come fully awake before he spoke.

"When?" he asked.

She knew the rest of the question. Lying there, she stretched languidly before rolling to face him. "I do not know," she said, as sadness crept into her voice. "And I am sorry that this is not such a relationship as you and I might desire."

His smile was wistful. "We each have our work," he said. "This must be enough for us."

"For now. One cannot know the future." Except one can, she added silently, thinking again of Bhopal and the pesticide plant. Even as that thought occurred, she wondered how Atasi and Naveen were getting on.

Halder drew back a little. "You were far away."

"I was," she agreed, but did not elaborate. A shy look crossed her face as she thought of one more guilty pleasure to indulge in before leaving. "Would you like to save water in the shower?" she asked him.

* * *

In Public Records, Atasi Patel received frowns of disapproval even before she broached her request to see copies of the permits and applications submitted by Union Carbide to construct the Bhopal pesticide plant. Aside from on harried clerk in an office, she was as far as she could tell the only woman in the place. That she was in fact a two-time award-winning journalist carried no weight here. The frown from the registrar clerk deepened further when he finally understood what she wanted to look at. His name was Deepak, and he looked as if he had lived his entire life in Public Records. Atasi wondered how much further he had to go to retire.

After almost an hour of waiting and haggling and waiting and displaying her newspaper creds for *The Times of India*, an underling led her in a roundabout way toward a viewing room, where several files had been stacked unevenly on a flimsy folding table fronted by a metal folding chair. She issued no complaint, but closed the door on the underling and set herself to work. Most of the files were in disarray, and she was forced to spend half of her two hours of viewing in arranging them in some sort of chronological order. Scrambling madly, she jotted as many notes as she could, taking moments to frown in disbelief at some of those she had written. If only Nakushi were here as Bombay Sapphire, she might apply some of those powers of knowledge that Agni had bestowed on her to make some sense out of what she was reading.

As it was, Atasi had the horrible suspicion that local government administrators in Bhopal were fully aware of the lethal dangers of methyl isocyanate, yet permitted Union Carbide to work with that gas with only nominal Indian oversight. In other words, there were hardly any safety controls established for the use of the gas. That in itself could only lead, eventually, to catastrophe...as Atasi already knew would transpire.

Almost nauseous, Atasi sat back in the chair, and felt one of the legs yield. Quickly she snagged the edge of the table to stabilize herself, and stood up just before the chair folded to one side. For women only, she thought, looking down at it without amusement. Somehow she would manage to mention this little incident in her report.

A few names appeared in the documents. She reviewed them once more to make certain that she had jotted them down, along with any of their titles mentioned. She was just finishing up when the underling returned, opened the door without knocking, and announced the end of her two hours.

Toward late afternoon Atasi found Naveen standing just inside an opening in a tall fence of bamboo around the yard of a house some seventy meters from the gate guard. Well-hidden from observation by the guard and, generally, from the plant, he managed to swing his camera out every once in a while, click a photograph, and tug himself back into shelter before anyone noticed. He hissed at Atasi when she passed by, and she joined him there.

"What are you doing here?" she asked. "This is a private residence."

"I told them who I was and what I wanted to do," Naveen explained. "She was happy to know that someone was investigating what she called 'the smells.' I haven't smelled anything yet, though."

"Maybe it only comes out at night," offered Atasi.

"That's possible. I'll come back here tonight for the samples. After that, I'd feel a lot more comfortable away from Bhopal. Atasi...this is a place of evil."

"We already know that," she shot back.

Subdued, he added, "I've gotten a couple shots of black vehicles, and a few shots of the passengers as they stepped out. Most were wearing suits, but I don't know any of them. Two were English, or American."

"American, more likely," said Atasi. "It is an American corporation. Here for cheap labor," she finished bitterly.

"One colonialist replaces another." He lofted a black eyebrow. "What did you find out?"

Atasi hesitated. The answers weren't clear to her. "I'm sure I found some useful information," she told him. "But as to what it means, I-I just don't know. We need someone who understands these matters."

"Your father."

She nodded. "He'll find someone."

"Step back," said Naveen, as a black vehicle pulled out of the compound. Its windows were tinted, but he aimed the camera at the rear license plate, and seemed satisfied with the shot and the angle from which he had taken it. "I think that's the third different plate," he told her. "It will be interesting to learn who the vehicles are registered to."

"Someone with more allowance than we get," said Atasi wryly.

He began putting away his camera and attachments. "Let's get back to the hotel. I'll come back later when it's dark."

"*We* will," she amended. "Just in case you need help."

*   *   *

With a sad heart Bombay Sapphire returned to Yawal Wildlife Sanctuary to resume her vigil for poachers of animals and timber. The interlude with Neelam had proved to be exactly what she needed. It had to end for the moment—she understood that, but she did not have to like it. Only her service to Agni signified more than the relationship with Halder.

Now, ensconced on a bed of banyan some ten meters above the forest floor, she waited and listened. Presently, to the rhythms of the jungle, Bombay Sapphire dozed off.

The voices reached her before the men who spoke them. Around her the forest had fallen quiet. Motionless, she scanned the jungle floor for them and found them just entering a small clearing: three men dressed in khaki, with rifles shouldered and plastic canteens dangling from web belts. The man wearing the yellow pith helmet seemed to be in charge. Perhaps twenty years older, his tan suggested that he had long ago left England for India. His once-yellow hair had been bleached white. He raised a hand, and the two men behind him stopped.

The second man, of darker Indian stock, cocked an ear to listen, but held still. The third man complained.

"Jeez, Sir Edward, what is it now?" he whined.

Sir Edward made sharp chopping gestures with his free hand, a demand for silence. A minute later, he shook his head impatiently. "It's nothing," he said softly. "Something in the trees. Langurs, maybe. We push on."

Bombay Sapphire was uncomfortably aware that she was attired in blue against a backdrop of green and every other color except blue. She held perfectly still and hoped none of them would look up. Her dark blue eyes followed their every movement until the men passed from view.

Silently she sat up, her face awash in curiosity. The name that had been spoken rang no bells for her, yet he was certainly familiar with the country and very probably with this territory. She had not expected that someone in British peerage might be involved in poaching—she would have to tread carefully here—but she had been sent to protect Yawal Sanctuary, and Agni had not mentioned any exceptions.

She dropped to the ground and followed in the direction the men had taken. As quiet and careful as they were, she discovered herself rather adept at reading trail signs. Footprints, of course, and grass once trod that had yet to straighten. A stem bent or broken, a twig crushed where someone stood, a few random hairs caught on leaves. She had to follow with caution, because the jungle was dense enough in places to conceal the men but a few meters ahead. Sound in those places was easier to detect, but visually she might as well have been wearing a mask.

Dew from fronds left their marks on Bombay Sapphire as she made her way through the trees and vines, and she began to watch the broad leaves more closely for signs of human passage. Here and there the dew was smeared. She reached the point where she was close enough to Sir Edward and his party that when the denizens fell silent during their passage, the silence included her as well.

The terrain began to change. Where it had been relatively flat, it was now riven with narrow rills now dry for the season, and unruly terrain hidden under thick grass. Anticipating that this would slow the party, Bombay Sapphire held back. It was tempting to fly for an overhead view of the ground, in the hope of locating them precisely, but that location would do her little good. So far the men had not done anything except enter the Sanctuary without permission; she wanted to know their purpose in coming here. She had to see.

Beside a vast banyan network she paused, and climbed up into it. Through the thinner foliage there she was able to make out an open, rolling field interspersed with single trees and covered by ferns, shrubs, and vines. Movement along the south perimeter of the field resolved itself into three men, now led by the Indian, who apparently was acting as a guide. Trailing him, the man who had complained earlier now continued to remonstrate with Sir Edward, who was struggling to ignore him.

Bombay Sapphire kept them in sight while she sat back and considered. All the while, she was losing ground to them. To catch them up, she would have to risk flight, for there was no way for her to cross the field without being spotted, especially not as her blue self. To transform to Nakushi for crossing might put her human self at risk: once bitten, by a cobra or krait, she had no idea whether transforming back to Bombay Sapphire would save her, or would prevent her from ever again becoming Nakushi.

The three men reached the far perimeter of the field. The Indian probed for passageways, and seemed to find something to his satisfaction. But the men did not re-enter the jungle. Instead, they studied the ground at their feet and around them, and the complainer used a stick to poke at something. Bombay Sapphire had no idea what it could be. It got the men's attention, however, and they cleared a small area and sat down, removing their backpacks and opening them—to what end, she was unable to see from her vantage point.

Still, as long as the men were not about to leave, she decided simply to remain where she was and to watch them. In the meantime, she kept her senses tuned. She was too far away to hear their voices, but there might be others in the area, as well as other denizens in the trees. Even as this last occurred to her, she felt a touch at her left elbow. A small hand had landed there. Turning slowly, she found that she had been joined by a black-faced gray langur, a female with an orange-haired infant still suckling. The langur seemed to have no fear of her. Bombay Sapphire tried a smile, as if that were a universal greeting between primates, but the only response was the hand now plucking at the tights over her elbow. Finally the langur drew up to a sitting position, tail hanging down past the limb, and seemed content to remain there.

The other members of a small troupe gathered around Bombay Sapphire there. She began to wonder whether she represented some sort of protection to them. Their natural enemies were tigers, smaller predators, and pythons, as well as a few raptors who sought to catch a langur out in the open. In the banyan, the most likely danger came from pythons, and from time to time she examined her arboreal surroundings for them. But the langurs were equally as alert, and might well detect one before she did.

What's going on, Agni? she thought wryly.

The sound she heard in response might have been a chuckle.

The men rose, without their backpacks, and began to spread out a little to three points of a triangle. The Indian reached down, apparently to make an adjustment, and Bombay Sapphire spotted a thick sheaf of what appeared to be meter-long dark grass as he shifted it. Bait, she concluded. But for what?

Even as she asked herself, the men faded into the jungle. She tested the wind; assuming it was the same as that around her, light and from the southwest, the men were downwind, not easily detected by whatever they sought to ensnare.

She glanced at the female langur and raised a blue eyebrow in a question. The langur seemed to shrug, as if to express ignorance. "Anthropomorphism," muttered Bombay Sapphire, wondering where the word had come from—the attribution of human gestures and behavior to animals. "Like trust," she added. "They seem unafraid of me."

The sun continued to filter through foliage and heat them. An intermittent breeze did little to cool them. Bombay Sapphire had no need of water, but the langurs seemed to be growing uncomfortable. Presently a few of them sought lower branches, where it might be shadier. The men did not reappear.

Still, there was no question in her mind now that Sir Edward and his team meant to trap something that frequented the path they had taken. She had to get closer; to do that, she had to go around to a spot behind the men. Staying low to the trees, she flew, with the echoes of the langurs' surprised chittering in her ears. Moments later she was standing on a thick branch that overlooked the spot where the men had set the trap. Still, she was unable to see the device, nor was there any sign of Sir Edward. But she was now close enough to act when the time came.

A tiny movement off to her right got her attention. The Indian man was there with a machete. To improve his view, he had taken a swipe at a vine. A white hand grabbed him and pulled him back, Sir Edward disapproving of the unnecessary movement.

"It's hot out here. Where is it?"

Bombay Sapphire recognized the voice of the complainer, and easily imagined him wiping sweat from his face with a handkerchief. Apparently the creature was due to make this round at this time. As a chronic whiner, however, the man might object to any inconvenience. *You can't rush prey*, she thought. She moved to a higher branch, one that gave her a better view of the open field. Nothing was moving out there. Smaller animals knew that the open space made them vulnerable to flying predators. The target had to be something larger. A tiger, a rhinoceros? An elephant? And did the men mean to capture it or kill it? Not that it mattered which; poaching was poaching.

Presently Bombay Sapphire heard it, a great beast pushing its way between saplings. It emerged from the tree line and clung to it as it began to make its way around the field. An elephant. *Her* elephant.

Now she had Sir Edward and his men located. From the high branch she dropped down, landing next to the Indian, whom she bowled over. A flash kick rendered him unconscious. The complainer dropped to his knees and began to beg incoherently. She grabbed Sir Edward's rifle—a .458 Marlin easily capable of bringing down an elephant —and bent the barrel. Even as he lodged a protest, she reached out to his collar and shook him. His head lolled with the violence of her efforts.

At this moment the complainer decided to make a run to safety. A hard sweep of her leg against his feet made him pitch forward to the grass and dirt. His head struck a tree trunk, and he lay still.

"What do you think you are doing?" yelled Sir Edward, as he struggled in vain to free himself. "Do you know who I am?"

"I don't care who you are," Bombay Sapphire said softly. "You're not killing that elephant, or any other animal. This is a protected Sanctuary. You've no business with weapons here."

"You ruined my rifle."

She slapped his face. "Focus, Sir Edward. The rifle is nothing compared to what I can do to you."

"You are going to regret this," he replied, still angry.

She sighed, and shook her head. He still wasn't getting it. She considered flying them to the mountain temple. The weight of the three men together was far less than the boulders she dropped on the Chinese tanks two years ago, but the men themselves were unwieldy to carry. The Indian man was not the problem. Still holding onto Sir Edward, she told him to leave the Sanctuary immediately. After a brief look into her eyes, he fled. The complainer was still out; she decided to leave him where he had fallen. Either he would make his way out of the sanctuary, or he might meet his fate in it.

"Why were you hunting that elephant?" she asked Sir Edward.

"Those tusks are worth a lot of money," he answered, as if she should have known.

"I know a remote tribe that would extract all your teeth and engrave them with ornate designs before stringing them on a necklace," she said. "It's tempting to take you to them, and hope you like porridge."

Without another word, she flew straight up with him. Leveling off after two miles, she headed for the mountain temple. At first, he kicked and screamed, and she almost dropped him. Already he had lost his pith helmet. After reassuring him that she would neither drop him nor kill him, he settled down. He looked nauseous, as if heights gave him vertigo.

"What," he began, and tried again. "What are you going to do with me?"

She did not respond. Air rushing past them tousled his hair and dried his eyes. He made fists, but did not attempt to strike her. His muscles stiffened in her arms, and she adjusted his position to make it easier for her to control him and carry him. Ahead loomed the great Himalayas and her destination. Higher into the air she rose. Sir Edward was struggling to breathe, so she dropped a couple thousand feet where there was more air for him.

"Where?" But the one word was all he could manage.

"We are flying north," she told him.

"Why?" Now his voice was stronger, as if he were coming to grasp his circumstances. Obviously she had no plans to drop him to his death, or she would have already done so.

"My task is to protect the Sanctuary that you and your men have violated," she said. "I would have protected any elephant or any animal from you, but that elephant was one I had rescued from a trap, probably set by men you had hired."

He did not respond to this, and she understood it to mean that he had in fact hired the trappers.

"Others hunt for tusks," he said bravely. "For ivory. And not only elephants. And not only for tusks. Each year seals are clubbed to death for their fur. Tigers are hunted for rugs. You cannot stop all of us."

"That is probably true," said Bombay Sapphire. "But I can stop you."

She released him. Screaming in shock and terror, he plummeted toward the ground. After a few seconds she dove after him, catching him a couple hundred meters above a rocky outcrop. His breathing was audible—rapid and shallow, and his heart rate accelerated. Gasping, he was unable to speak as she rose to her previous altitude. His body was slack in her arms, and for a moment she thought he had passed out. But his eyes were open and focused. He seemed to want to say something, but was unable to speak.

She expanded on an answer she had given him earlier. "I'm taking you to a mountain temple in Himachal Pradesh, near Shimla," she said. "It is very cold. You may wish to take shelter there. Whether you do or do not makes no difference to me. If you return to Yawal Sanctuary, I shall fly you there again, and this time drop you off from about two miles up."

"You won't get away with this," he threatened.

"'Get away'? You are the one breaking the law. I am merely enforcing it."

"You can't do this—"

"Be silent," she ordered. "Or I shall drop you again."

They arrived at the Buddhist temple amid the soaring snowcapped peaks. After setting him down, she searched him—roughly, for he struggled against her—and extracted his Palmetto, leaving him incommunicado. Without another word, she rose straight into the air, and bent her course back toward the south.

008

In the dark, Atasi and Naveen huddled close together, where they could see the guard shack and the entrance to the compound. Light jackets protected them from the chill air. Naveen had traded his camera and related equipment for a small metal box, cushioned on the inside, and containing several capped vials for collecting samples. There was no activity inside the shack, and the few street lights were not working.

Naveen tagged her. "Wait here," he instructed, and dashed across the street to the area of sparse and dying grass outside the perimeter fence. After he had gone a few meters, Atasi was no longer able to see him. She hoped this indicated that anyone watching from the guard shack would also be unable to see him.

Waiting made her nervous. A vehicle backfired on a nearby street, and she stepped back, startled, while her heart slowed. Across the street there came no sound from Naveen. Six samples, he had said. That was all the vials he could locate. She counted seconds. How long could it take to collect six samples?

The sound of running footsteps alerted her. The shape of Naveen came into view. In that moment, the light came on in the guard shack. A man yelled, "Halt." Atasi was unable to see him, but assumed he was the duty guard. She caught Naveen by the elbow, and together they dashed away. The guard began firing his sidearm. Naveen stumbled and fell.

Atasi dropped to her knees beside him. "Are you...?" she gasped.

He thrust the metal box at her. "I've had it," he croaked, coughing. With the cough, a warm liquid splashed on Atasi's arm. "Take it. Get...away. Get our stuff and...get on the...the train."

"I won't leave you," she cried.

"You can't, can't save me. I know. Go! Save the...story!"

Atasi heard running. She straightened, eyes streaming tears, and fled around the corner to another street. A dull street lamp lit their vehicle. She got in, started the engine, and wheeled the car around just as someone appeared at the top of the street and fired his weapon after her. She heard a sharp *clunk* as a bullet struck the rear of the car. In defense she began to swerve the car from one side of the street to the other and back again. She heard no more metallic impacts. Gaining a main road, she sped back toward their hotel.

* * *

Bombay Sapphire paused on her journey south to spend the darkness of night on the tree platform hard by the new shrine to Agni. As she expected, Agneya soon joined her there. She had long held the suspicion that the boy was an extension of the god of storms; but this was not something she would dare inquire of him. Instead, she often listened to his advice.

After she landed on the platform, he showed up so quickly that he might have anticipated her arrival. Munching a mango, he settled in beside her, saying nothing, listening as she was to the night. She was glad of the familiar face, and of the company. When it came time to speak, Agneya broke the silence.

"There has been a death," he said, in a voice as quiet as starlight.

Bombay Sapphire's heart fluttered against her ribs. Not Atasi, please not Atasi.

"It is Naveen, her photographer."

That's just as bad, she thought. "How?"

"Atasi is in the Grande Hotel, Room 127," he replied. "She will check out in the morning." With that, he finished the mango, and slipped down from the tree.

Night flight normally was a pleasure for Bombay Sapphire. Now, racked by worry for her best friend, she sped through the darkness, watchful only for the blinking lights that indicate an aircraft. Far below, a few headlights, no larger than the eyes of gnats, illuminated rural roadways. She flew the direct route, to the northwest and the state of Madhya Pradesh, to Bhopal. As she reached the city limits, she descended gradually, choosing to fly over the darker areas, where people were more likely to be sleeping.

Arriving just past the hotel, she slipped into an alley and, after looking this way and that, transformed back to Nakushi. The hotel clerk paid no attention to her as she entered and made for the staircase. The steps creaked even under her slight weight. At Room 127 she rapped lightly on the door, and listened.

There was no response at first. Presently she detected a sniffling, as if someone were trying to stop a flow of tears. Nakushi tested the door, and found it locked.

"Atasi," she said, just loud enough to be heard in the room.

No sound of footsteps reached her, but a long moment later the door opened, just a crack, and half of Atasi's tear-reddened face appeared. Recognition was immediate: she yanked the door open and threw herself against Nakushi, clinging to her to keep from drowning. Nakushi half-carried her inside, and nudged the door closed with her foot.

Once inside, Atasi broke down in tears again. In a shaking voice, her thin body trembling, she told Nakushi all that had transpired, including Naveen's insistence that she save herself and the story.

"I left him there to die," she wailed, her grief a punctuation to end her tale.

Nakushi tried to comfort her. "I don't see what else you could have done," she said gently. "You would have been in danger, had you remained. And I doubt the police would have looked kindly upon what you and Naveen were doing. Union Carbide is too big and too important to Bhopal."

Atasi could only nod.

They drifted to the bed and sat down. Atasi wiped her eyes on the bed cover. Nakushi did not know what else to say to her. Struggling for words, she returned to their visit into the future.

"You and I know what is going to happen, years from now," she said. "The task before you is to reduce the effects of the disaster, or perhaps even to prevent it altogether."

"Naveen will, will get a byline," said Atasi. She expelled a long sigh. "Nakushi, I'm frightened. They may still be looking for me. We didn't try to hide the fact of our presence. We, I, can be traced here eventually. I'm going to take the early bus toward Bombay."

"I have a much better idea," said Nakushi. "Gather up your things, and the samples that Naveen took."

Atasi brightened a little. "Oh, yes, I get to fly with you."

"Just don't look down," Nakushi advised. "*Ashmita.*"

* * *

Dawn was lifting the cover of darkness from the great city by the time Bombay Sapphire landed at the Patel estate and acquired the attention of one of the servants. He in turn immediately went to notify Dayaram Patel, Atasi's uncle as well as sponsor for her job with *The Times of India*. Atasi's wind-blown hair needed attention, and she went into a water closet to see to it. Bombay Sapphire opted against a resumption of her Nakushi persona. Dayaram Patel knew much about her, and was not about to tell anyone, or to allow his staff and servants to betray information.

In less than a minute Patel reached the reception room where Bombay Sapphire awaited him. Although she had not seen him for the better part of a year, he had changed but little, a small, thin man not quite her height, attired in an off-white leisure suit that fit him as if he had been born in it and to it. Silver highlighted his full dark hair, and his angular face bore a mix of concern for Atasi and pleasure at seeing Bombay Sapphire once more.

A gesture from him sent Bombay Sapphire to a plush chair, while he took up residence on the sofa. He looked as if he had so many questions that he scarcely knew where to begin. Bombay Sapphire rescued him with the same tale that Atasi had told her.

When she had finished, Patel was aghast. "You actually went into the future?" he said, amazed.

"I am certain that we were cast there by Agni," she told him. "I do not believe that I have the power of time-travel."

"Yes, of course. Still..."

She smiled. "I know."

"And this happened at Bhopal," he said. "Uncounted thousands." He mulled this over some more. Finally he spread his hands, a gesture of helplessness. "What can we do? Union Carbide has many friends in the government. It provides jobs for our people. It is highly respected in the business community. There will be a stubborn opposition to any sort of conjecture we might offer."

"You can print the truth," Bombay Sapphire told him. "Put them on the defensive. Make them prove that what you print is wrong. Put out a call for samples, to be collected by an impartial committee and analyzed in an independent laboratory. If someone in the government objects, report that as well. Publicity could force Union Carbide to take the steps necessary to prevent these toxic leaks."

"Are you having a nice chat?" asked Atasi, returning from her ministrations. She sat down at the other end of the sofa. "*Appa*," she said, addressing Patel as father even though he was her uncle, "Naveen was killed there. He was not trespassing, or doing anything illegal..."

"I know," he said. "I know."

Her eyes moistened. "He insisted that I leave him behind. *Appa*, he lived with his parents, and his pay helped to support them." She fixed her gaze on Patel, leaving the request unspoken.

"They will be taken care of, *Betee*," he said. "I'll speak with the Managing Editor."

"*Sukria, Appa.*"

"If I may," said Bombay Sapphire. At a gesture of permission from Patel, she continued. "Union Carbide will have already identified Naveen. It will not take them long to find out about Atasi. I myself have a task from Agni, and must leave. It might be useful to have Atasi live here, and to have a bodyguard whenever she goes out. It might also be useful to have private guards at Atasi's cottage and at Naveen's apartment, in the event that someone shows up from Union Carbide."

"I agree," said Patel. "It will be arranged this day."

"You should also inform your editor," said Bombay Sapphire, to Atasi. She got up and headed for the back entrance. "I'll be back when I can," she said. "One more thing. Do you happen to know of a Sir Edward?"

"Sir Edward Willoughby," Patel replied. "He has lived in India for the better part of four decades." His eyes narrowed. "Why?"

"I caught him poaching elephants in Yawal Wildlife Sanctuary," she told him. "That might be newsworthy."

"If the *Times* will publish such a crime," cautioned Atasi. "I've heard of him. Sir Edward is something like Union Carbide. He is too important to touch."

"Perhaps he would reveal something in an interview. Atasi, I have to go. I will be back."

Atasi rushed to her for a parting hug.

009

Once back inside the Sanctuary, Bombay Sapphire found a comfortable position in a banyan tree and keened her ears to the sounds of the tropical forest. A brief practice enabled her to ignore the squawks of birds and the chittering of monkeys, and to focus on any human voices and activity she might detect. But the forest was relatively quiet. She waited for half an hour, and took to the air in a proactive search for poachers.

Sunlight glistened on the rich green leaves as she passed overhead. Here and there, openings in the canopy caught her eye, and she hovered to inspect each one for activity below. But there were no other people about; probably it was too hot and humid for them. In one glade she spotted a tiger resting in the shrubs, out of sight in the cool shade. She heard, rather than saw, an elephant. A troop of monkeys was foraging in the trees for fruit and flowers. As she resumed her flight, she wondered how long Agni intended for her to maintain her vigil. Surely there were other tasks she might attend to.

Eventually she came across another suitable banyan tree, this one spreading under the canopy and in the shade. She dropped down; here it was cooler—not that temperature affected her, but she gained the impression of cooler air around her, and that was comforting. A network of limbs supported her as she stretched out, face down, to observe the glade that opened to her right. With the heat of the day blanketing the glade, most of the animals had retreated to the shelter and shade of the forest. She shut one eye and one ear and allowed herself to doze off.

Pelting rain brought her awake. She wiped the water from her eyes, sat up, and keyed her senses to her surroundings. Surely nothing would be out hunting in this storm—not tiger, not python, not man—for just as surely the prey would have taken shelter. Rain did not affect her, of course; even her blue tights and wraparound remained dry, water beading on the fabric and rolling off without effect. She took off for another aerial search of the Sanctuary.

Nobody was hunting in the rain. She was just about to call it a day when she spotted the jeep parked among the trees and partially covered with broken branches of shrubbery. Nearby ran a path worn by sambar and chital; the former was on the United Nations endangered list. If hunters were lying in wait for one...

Worried, Bombay Sapphire began to expand her search. The sambar was an all-weather deer. It might seek shelter from a heavy downpour, a monsoon, but otherwise ran carefree. She had to fly low, under the canopy, to spot the hunting blind. If she could see them, they could see her—not that it would do them much good. But she wanted to catch the hunters in the act, without harm to the deer.

Branches and leaves moved below her, an effect of the rain, but largely indistinguishable from movements caused by hunters. A bird fluttered, changing perches for better protection. Grass moved with the passing of a snake, possibly a cobra.

The report from the rifle reached her at the same time a bullet struck her chest. Quickly she caught the bullet before it could fall to the forest floor, and tucked it into a pocket of her tights for examination later. Where had it come from? Who had fired it? She saw no one below, no sign of anyone. But they had seen her. She flew to the shelter of a tall tree to think while she kept watch.

Possibly the hunters were unaware that she could not be harmed. Try as she might, she could think of no other reason for them to open fire and thereby expose their presence. But now that she knew they were in the area, it was imperative that she locate them before they killed a sambar.

The rain showed no sign of letting up. The sky, overcast from horizon to horizon, promised a gloomy day with poor visibility. Again she flew, this time slowly, and staying at or above the canopy, her eyes intent on what she was able to see of the ground. They had to be somewhere.

Bombay Sapphire decided to check the deer path, from one end to the other. If the hunters were after sambar or chital, they would have to be where they had a clear shot. Still above the canopy, she traced the path to where it merged into denser wood, the trees so thick that a human could not fit between them. Reversing her direction, she followed the path to where she had been shot...

There! Just there. The green of camouflage fabric, in contrast to the green of vegetation. They had not spotted her this time, else they might have fired again. She did not want to dive down and risk scattering them. Stealth would be required.

The crunch of a dry twig and the rustle of leaves alerted her to the path. A chital—she spotted it fifty meters up the path, slowly making its way to its doom. She hovered above it, drifting when it moved. Lightly built, it stood perhaps a meter high at the shoulder. A multitude of white spots dotted its orange-brown fur. Atop its head was a rack at least a meter wide—an ideal trophy for a hunter.

"No," Bombay Sapphire hissed to herself.

Now she had no choice. Swooping over the trees, she dropped to the ground well behind the hunting blind. From this angle she was able to make out the shapes of three individuals, almost certainly men. The long sticks in their hands had to be rifles.

She crept toward them, avoiding twigs and dry leaves, and gently pushing past thin branches that obstructed her way.

Ten meters, five. Not rifles, but walking sticks to ward off snakes from their path. Wide-eyed, she halted. One of the three was a woman with a...film camera.

"O Agni," murmured Bombay Sapphire, relieved. "What I almost did."

She held her position, knowing the chital was close. One man held a camera, while the other seemed to be taking notes, possibly regarding time and location. None of them moved except to jot a word or two. She could hear the faint sounds of the chital as it approached; evidently the nature students could as well. She heard their sharp intake of breath as the chital stepped into view. The soft whirr of the camera alerted the deer, and for a moment it stood completely still, searching only with its eyes and nose.

Two minutes later, satisfied with its safety for the moment, the chital continued along the path. But minute clicks from the stills camera alerted it. Bombay Sapphire heard the beast crash through the vegetation; one of the men swore mildly, disappointed. Quietly Bombay Sapphire retreated, and took to the air when she was well out of hearing distance. A minute later, she had taken refuge once more in a banyan.

After night enveloped the forest, Bombay Sapphire flew back to Bombay, there to settle onto the platform in the banyan tree that grew outside the newly-dedicated shrine to Agni. As she expected, Agneya soon joined her. She was virtually certain now that the boy was a physical manifestation of the god of storms. It was not in her to ask for confirmation. He seemed to regard her presence this night as in the natural order of things. Yet he seemed sad.

She asked Agneya about this, but he merely shrugged and looked away. There were only a few major concerns on her mind, and she broached two of them. "Bhopal? Or is it my sister, Savitra?"

Agneya did not respond at first. Something far out into the night held his attention. She was unable to determine its nature. It might have been anything from a mugging to a nightbird snagging a flying insect. Without looking at her, at last he whispered a single word. "Savitra."

Bombay Sapphire's heart skipped a couple of beats. What had happened? "What about her?" she asked carefully, not certain that she really wanted to know.

"She has been arrested."

Shock and dismay fought for Bombay Sapphire's attention, and both won. At first, she did not know what to say. Her little sister, jailed? In retrospect she might have guessed this would happen eventually. But the circumstances were not ordinary. The demon Kallia was supposed to be protecting

Savitra. Unless there was some underlying purpose in having her jailed, Kallia would not have allowed her detention.

"Where is she?" asked Bombay Sapphire.

"In the police station by the river."

"Like the Black Hole of Calcutta."

"She has a small window looking out over the canal," Agneya told her.

Frowning, she eyed him in the dark. "You've been there?"

"No."

Heart weary, she got to her feet on the platform, and took off into the night without a word.

The flight to the police station was simple enough, even in the dark. There was enough ambient light for her to locate it. For a while she hovered well above the river and away from the stink of it, until she was able to locate the window of Savitra's cell. As she had anticipated, the cell was actually below river level, although an elevated walkway kept the water out of the cells. She picked out a place to stand, and peered between the bars into the dark.

"Did you come to gloat?" Savitra rasped.

"How often do the guards come by?" asked Bombay Sapphire.

"I don't know," her sister whined. "How would I know?"

"You count them as they pass your cell."

"Why bother?"

Bombay Sapphire glanced around. No one else was about at this time of night. A boat passed by on the river, its ringing bell the only sound other than the lapping of the water against the walkway. A brief examination of the window told her that it was not large enough for Savitra to slip through.

"Why did you come?" asked Savitra.

"You are my *chhotee bahan*. My little sister. Of course I came, once I found out. What are you charged with?"

Savitra shook her head. "They have not said." She plucked at her office suit, now no longer white, and moaned. "Look at me. Look at what they've done to my clothes."

"That should be the least of your worries, Savitra. You can always buy more clothes."

Now she examined the cell. Her sister was the sole occupant. She nodded to herself: fewer complications and noise. With hardly any effort at all, she ripped the iron bars from the stones that held them. Seeing what she was about, Savitra tried to crawl through the window. Bombay Sapphire stopped her.

"Let me move some of these stones first," she said, and proceeded to do so.

Casting several of them into the river, she cleared an opening far larger than Savitra needed to fit through. Gently but firmly Bombay Sapphire tugged at Savitra's forearms, while her feet scrabbled again the inside of the wall. Finally she was clear of the cell. Without a word Bombay Sapphire scooped her up and flew off with her into the night.

At first, Savitra's eyes were squeezed shut. She dared not look out or, especially, down. Gradually she became accustomed to the air blowing past her and risked cracking one eyelid halfway open.

"I won't let you fall," promised Bombay Sapphire. "I would never let you fall."

Savitra licked her lips, but the breeze quickly dried them. "Where are we going?"

"To Dharavi, *choti*, where we used to live. Remember the banyan tree, and the platform? We're going there."

Savitra looked down at the lights of Bombay, and stiffened. A tiny scream escaped her, as if she had just seen a mouse crawl over her foot.

"It's all right, *choti*. You won't fall."

"Va...*vahaan kyon*? Why there?"

"It will be safe," said Bombay Sapphire. "We can talk there."

"T-talk?"

"About how you ended up in jail."

"Oh. That."

"Almost there," said Bombay Sapphire. "We're going down now."

Bombay Sapphire gently lowered Savitra to the platform. Together they sat down, dangling their legs over the side. She quelled the urge to transform back to Nakushi. Whatever she felt for her sister at the moment, complete trust was not a part of it. But the affection remained, nevertheless.

"It is a warm night," Savitra said absently, as she looked about, anywhere but at her. "What have you been up to, Nakushi?" she asked.

It was a perfunctory question, and she guessed that Savitra was using it to avoid other topics. She gave her sister a truthful answer. "Agni sent me to protect a wildlife sanctuary from poachers."

Savitra thought about that. A light laugh escaped her. "There cannot be much money in that," she said at last.

"Not for the money, *choti*, but for the good and the service."

"I never cared for tiger-skin rugs."

"But *choti*, you have one in your office," Bombay Sapphire reminded her.

"It is Kallia's."

"How *is* that black demon these days?"

That question garnered a long silence. Bombay Sapphire waited, patiently yet on edge. She had gotten to the crux of the matter, and now felt that Savitra was on the verge of a turning point. But the girl had to turn on her own; she would resist encouragement.

The sounds of the night picked up. Insects and birds; a dog barked desultorily.

Someone yelled. The honk of a horn protested a traffic offense.

"She betrayed me," whispered Savitra.

Bombay Sapphire nodded glumly; she had expected something like that. It saddened her that Savitra had not. "Then I have two questions, *choti*. First, how?"

Under the smudged office shirt, Savitra's shoulders stiffened first, then slumped in resignation. Her voice was as quiet as the night had been. "She said she had arranged a pickup for the Dholes," she began. "An amount of opium. I would have left that to a...well, I guess to Dimmy, who had been assigned..." She drew a deep breath and let half of it out. "Kallia said the courier insisted on turning the shipment over to me; he trusted no one else. It sounded...reasonable."

"So you went," said Bombay Sapphire.

"As soon as the package was in my hands, the police emerged from hiding places. I had no chance. Kallia had called them, probably anonymously. There was no one else who could have done it."

Bombay Sapphire had anticipated an explanation of this nature. But the critical question came next. "All right. Why, Savitra?"

In the dark, Savitra began to tremble. Presently the tears fell, and choked her voice. She struggled to speak. Bombay Sapphire rested a hand on her back, intending it as a comfort. Savitra leaned into her, and wept.

Her lips moved soundlessly against the blue fabric, while Bombay Sapphire's arm now drew her tightly, protectively.

"I just...I just wanted nice things," Savitra bawled. "Just something nice. A clean sari. Food without...without the grit of the alley in it. A jewel. The...the power to have what I wanted, whatever I wanted."

"I know," whispered Bombay Sapphire.

"But it doesn't mean anything, it never meant anything. To have...just to have...it means *nothing*." She leaned her head back. Tear tracks lined her face, and moisture made her eyes glisten. "It never meant anything, did it? It was all just...just *things*."

"I know. And you lost who you were in the process."

Savitra slowly nodded. "Oh, what do I do, Nakushi?"

It was a question Bombay Sapphire dared not answer. Savitra had to find her own way. "What do you want to do, Savitra?" she rejoined.

"I-I-I don't, don't know. I don't know what to do. I want to get away." She fisted tears from her eyes, which only started them flowing again. "I have to leave. I have to run."

"From...the Dholes?"

"Yes." She nodded vigorously, spilling tears. "From them. From...her. Help me. Nakushi, help me!"

Ever so slightly, the tree quivered. Bombay Sapphire knew where to look. A moment later, the head of Agneya rose above the edge of the platform. He did not climb onto it, but instead slung a pair of blankets and two cushions at them. Bombay Sapphire paid him with a smile, and felt the tree again as he descended.

Bombay Sapphire spread the two blankets, then placed the pillows. "We'll sleep here tonight," she said. "In the morning..."

Savitra allowed herself to stretch out on a blanket. "Yes?"

"In the morning, we'll go see some people I know. Good night, *choti*. Get some sleep."

Bombay Sapphire laid back, smiled wistfully, and said, "Nakushi."

010

The report of Savitra's escape elicited a coarse shriek from Kallia. This in turn shattered windows and cracked frame wood and plaster, some of which fell on her from the ceiling. She met this disaster with curses that only the pantheon would understand. Meanwhile, the messenger who delivered the report cowered on his knees, and lowered his forehead to the carpet in front of Kallia's desk.

"*How?*" she screamed. "How could this happen?"

"The door was still locked, Sagacious One," said the messenger to the carpet. "The window, however..."

"*What about it?*"

"It was gone, O Dark Demon of the Deccan."

"Gone? What do you mean, gone? Speak!"

"The bars, the...the stone blocks, gone, all gone."

"Imbecile!" Kallia pointed a finger at him. A jagged yellow streak struck him on the leg. Smoke rose from the blackened spot as he writhed on the carpet. "She would have needed *tools*! She *couldn't* have... couldn't..."

Realization swept over Kallia as if Shiva himself had shaken her. "The blue witch," she whispered hoarsely. "She's still alive. It has to be her doing. Shiva said she...but she's still alive!" Kallia trembled with the effort she made to regain her composure. Her eyes lost some of their fire, and her fists unclenched. She sat down with exaggerated care on the chair at her desk.

"Get up, simpering fool," she ordered, and the messenger scrambled to his feet. "Find the blue witch. She is making news somewhere. She has been seen somewhere. Find out where and when. Learn what she was doing." She pointed, but no fire emerged. "Go!"

He dashed from the office and collided with the front door as he tried to open it. The impact split the skin on his forehead. Terror overwhelmed pain as he finally forced himself through the gap he had created.

* * *

As the sun rose, Nakushi awoke and stretched. Hope suffused her as she lotused her legs and watched Savitra sleeping. The girl needed clean clothing, but Nakushi was reluctant to leave her, lest she should awaken and find herself alone. Savitra needed to know that her rescue had not been a dream, and that she had already taken a step or two toward a potential recovery. She needed the reassurance of her older sister.

The platform creaked with the sudden arrival of additional weight. Nakushi turned around to find Daalachini, the *apsara*-in-training from Mount Meru, now sitting there. Although the supernatural girl had never seen Nakushi, she obviously knew who she was. Instead of lavender gossamer, she now wore a royal blue sari that set off her intensely-black hair to perfection. Blue sandals shod her feet. A ruby-red bindi stood out against the olive brown of her forehead.

"Agni has decreed that I am to serve you," she said.

Nakushi reached out to take her hand. "Daala? It is good to see you, but I don't understand. Agni sent you?"

"To serve you. To help you. But I am enjoined from fighting for you. That, you must do on your own."

"I...see. Very well." Nakushi dug out a sheaf of currency from her pocket and peeled off two hundred rupees. "Please bring us bowls of sauced vegetables and rice, Daala," she instructed. "And my sister needs a sari. Something subdued. Lemon yellow, I think. Or sky blue. Sandals to match."

"In what size?"

Nakushi grimaced and shrugged, and eyed Daala from head to toe. "I don't know. If it would fit you, it will fit her."

"Who are you talking to?" asked Savitra, rubbing sleep from her eyes as she sat up.

Daala flew straight up through the foliage...and vanished.

"You mean you didn't see her?"

"See who?" Savitra asked.

"Never mind. Food and fresh clothing will arrive shortly. How did you sleep, *choti*?"

"I-I don't know. I think I had bad dreams, but they are unclear to me."

"Perhaps that is just as well," was Nakushi's assessment.

"But I-I think I hurt you. And...and there was the aroma of *garam masala*."

Nakushi flashed a wry smile. "Probably the cinnamon."

"What does it mean?"

She withheld the truth from Savitra. "Maybe you were hungry."

Savitra rubbed her belly. "I *am* hungry."

Nakushi leaned back on braced arms. "It is good to hear your voice again, *choti*."

She looked away. "I have...done... things."

Tenderly, Nakushi touched her arm. "And you have stopped," she said quietly.

"Yes. But...they will look for me, you know."

"The police?"

"No," said Savitra. "I mean, yes, but... no, I meant the Dholes."

"There is a way to save you from both."

Savitra turned back. "Tell me!"

Again the platform trembled; food and clothing had arrived.

"I'll tell you on the way," said Nakushi.

An hour later, with the sun now halfway up the sky, they arrived at the Patel Estate. Following introductions, Dayaram Patel escorted them to a conference room. Inside, Atasi Patel was waiting for them, sitting in a chair at the side of the table. The table itself was empty of everything except Atasi's notebook, and glistened in the light from the three chandeliers. Bombay Sapphire sat down opposite Atasi, and motioned for an uncertain Savitra to take the chair next to her. Patel himself went to his accustomed seat at the head of the table.

Patel clapped his hands together once to signal the start of the conference. With his eyes on no one in particular, he said, in a familiar understatement, "I gather there's a problem."

As perhaps he had intended, the statement lightened the mood. Savitra actually laughed, though lightly.

Bombay Sapphire said, "Two nights ago, my sister Savitra was arrested and jailed on charges that have yet, as far as I'm aware, to be filed. Those charges involve the delivery and potential sale of opium."

The conference room door opened, and one of the estate's service staff pushed a cart inside, laden with a coffee pot, a tea pot, assorted cups and utensils, and a silver serving set for sugar and cream. There was also a bowl of fruit, a stack of cloth napkins, a stack of small ceramic plates, and a silver tray bearing squares of baklava. The servant distributed the napkins, poured coffee or tea as requested, and served the baklava. He left the cart behind as he backed out of the room.

Unable to hold back, Savitra grabbed a handful of small plums, but before she placed them on her plate, she dropped them back into the bowl. Daintily she picked one back up, plus an apricot.

"So they didn't feed you in jail," said Bombay Sapphire. But she said it lightly, not to give offense.

"Twice a day," she replied. "Rice and some vegetables. A moldy banana."

Spoons clinked as they stirred coffee or tea. Fastidious, Patel ate and drank slowly, his tongue catching all the nuances of flavor. It amused Bombay Sapphire to see that Atasi's eating habits mirrored his.

All the signs pointed to a working breakfast, so she said, to Patel, "I think you know that Savitra is the head of the Deccan Dholes. Was the head. She and I discussed her situation on the flight here. Please know that I speak for her now."

Patel made a generous sweep of his arm. "Go ahead, but I think I already know where this is going."

Bombay Sapphire smiled. "I would be astonished if you did not know. Incidentally, this is the best baklava I have ever tasted."

"It is home-grown," he said. "There is a small pistachio orchard on the estate."

"And fruit trees, Appa," said Atasi.

"Savitra is willing to tell everything she knows about the Deccan Dholes," Bombay Sapphire continued. "Names, locations, events. As far as she is concerned, her association with them is ended. In return for this information and for her testimony in court as needed, she is neither to be charged with any crimes, nor is she to be imprisoned. She wishes to return to a life with me, her sister, such as we are able to live it."

"I see," Patel said, chewing thoughtfully.

"One more thing," said Bombay Sapphire, before he could comment further. "Daala," she called out.

Immediately the *apsara*-in-training appeared in the conference room. Atasi gasped in shock, while Patel seemed to take the event in stride. On this occasion Daala was wearing a light green sari with matching sandals. She stood at the foot of the table, waiting for instructions.

"It's a long story that I'd rather not go into," said Bombay Sapphire. "But I will say that Daalachini was sent to me by Agni to assist me in any way I need. I want her to be present at this conference, and to have the same freedom of movement on the estate as the rest of us. Please, sir," she added heavily. "If you would advise your staff regarding her?"

"Of course," said Patel. After dabbing at his mouth with a napkin, he got to his feet. "I have a few telephone calls to make. Meanwhile, please enjoy your food and drink."

In Patel's absence, Savitra said shakily, "I'm nervous. And scared." She twisted to face her older sister. "What if he calls the police and turns me in?" she worried.

"Even if he cannot help you," Bombay Sapphire told her, "he would not turn you in. And in any case, I would get you out of here." She reached out and gave Savitra a reassuring hug. "We'll solve this together, *choti*."

"Yes, we will," added Atasi.

Daalachini stood by, hovering, until Bombay Sapphire gestured her to a chair. "You're part of this, too, Daala. Have some tea."

"What do you do?" Atasi asked her.

"I dance," Daalachini replied. "Sometimes I sing, or act characters. Or I bring food, or clear it away." She sighed and smiled. "I do what I am told. I do whatever is needed."

"She is an *apsara*," explained Bombay Sapphire. "Agni assigned her to me."

"An *apsara*-in-training," said Daala. "If I may have one of those dates?"

Savitra passed her the bowl. "So you are on our side."

"I am on her side," said Daala, indicating Bombay Sapphire. "And her friends are my friends."

"I'm her sister," Savitra corrected.

"Yes, I know. I have never had a sister. Or perhaps all *apsaras* are sisters. Brahma creates us, sometimes while he is sleeping." She thought for a moment and added, "I am a laukika *apsara*-in-training."

"You are of the world, then," said Bombay Sapphire.

"Perhaps that is why Agni sent me to you."

"Can you change shape?" Atasi asked.

Daalachini turned to her. "Do you not like my appearance?"

"Oh, it's not that. I am merely curious."

"I am in training," said Daala. "I am still learning my powers. For now, I am able to create clothing from my own body. This sari is a part of me, made from my skin."

"I wish I could do that," muttered Savitra.

"But think of all the shopping you would miss out on," said Atasi.

Dayaram Patel returned in the middle of their laughter. His arrival sobered their expressions. He returned to his place at the head of the table, folded his hands together and used them to push his plate away.

"I have spoken with several people by telephone," he began, primarily addressing Savitra. "In half an hour from now we shall begin to receive guests. Deputy Police Commissioner Aadav Rani. Deputy Public Prosecutor Maani Kumar. A court recorder." He turned briefly to Atasi. "And of course a reporter from *The Times of India*." He warmed his tea from the pot. "Now, Savitra, let us discuss what you are going to tell them."

011

In the event, Savitra told the police commissioner and the public prosecutor everything she knew about the Deccan Dholes, and included names, dates, and places as best she could remember them. She did not possess any documentation to corroborate her story—that was retained in a safe that only Kallia could open—but she did not need any. Those who listened to her, including the reporter, were quite capable of investigating the facts of her story.

But it was the question from the police commissioner, Aadav Rani, that changed the complexion of the interview. After Savitra had been exhausted of information, he turned to Bombay Sapphire and said, "Sir Edward Willoughby has filed a formal complaint against you. On his affidavit he states that you forcefully abducted him and took him to a remote location and left him there to die."

"I understand how that might be one interpretation of my actions," agreed Bombay Sapphire. "Yet his statement omits so much. For example, the fact that he was in the Yawal Wildlife Sanctuary poaching wild game—tigers, elephants, rhinos, whatever he and his team could find. The fact that when I abducted him, I stopped him in the act of shooting an elephant. The fact that I dropped him off just outside a monastery in the Himalayas." She paused briefly to smile at him. "I don't suppose he mentioned any of that, Commissioner?"

Rani's lips pursed as he scowled. For a few seconds he drummed his fingertips on the table. "And you would attest to all of this?" he asked.

"I would have to ask Agni," she replied after a moment. "Giving such testimony was not what he empowered me to do. So my answer to you is: provisionally, yes."

"Sir Edward is very...prominent," said Rani. "I'm sure you are aware of this. And I am told that your real name—"

"My *human* name, sir."

"Yes, of course. It is Nakushi. Nakushi Kulasingam."

Bombay Sapphire flashed him a hard look. Though she spoke courteously, there was a cold fury behind her words. "I'm not sure I care for what you are implying, sir."

Patel cleared his throat for attention. "Commissioner Rani is simply concerned regarding the ramifications of pursuing official charges against Sir Edward."

Bombay Sapphire stood up. "He should be more worried about having to pursue them against me." To Rani, she added, "Let me make this clear to you, Commissioner. Regardless of my personal human 'background,' I serve Agni, who empowers me to serve Bharat. I go where the wrongdoing takes me. Sir Edward was poaching. That is illegal. It is up to you to determine whether you wish to pursue this, but know this: if he resumes his poaching, I shall return him to the Himalayas."

"I have to add," Atasi broke in quickly, "that this story will appear in *The Times of India*."

"I would recommend against that, Miss Patel," Rani said heavily. "I am sure the *Times* would wish to avoid a lawsuit. Always assuming, of course, that your editor would want to publish such a story."

"What are you saying, sir?" Atasi threw back, her face as hard now as that of Bombay Sapphire.

"I think you understand very well what I am saying. Let us leave it at that." He turned to Savitra. "As regards your testimony, I will have an affidavit drawn up that contains your information, and you will sign it, and we will conduct an investigation. You will please remain available for further interviews."

Rani motioned to the Deputy Public Prosecutor and to the court reporter, neither of whom had spoken. "This meeting is now concluded. Dayaram," he said, with a nod to Patel. "I'll be in touch later, I'm sure."

In the aftermath, Bombay Sapphire fought to control her outrage. At least there had been no charges of breaking Savitra out of jail, or of Savitra escaping from jail. No charges yet, she amended, with a glance at Patel. Reluctantly, almost unwillingly, she sat back down after Rani and his team had departed. The conference was not something Agni had prepared her for. She found herself wishing he would intervene, or at least give her a few words of encouragement. Failing that, she looked to Dayaram Patel.

"I suppose this was to be expected," he said, trying to calm the storm in the room. "The involvement of Sir Edward has placed Commissioner Rani in a difficult position."

"That's too bad," Bombay Sapphire said icily. "But what do you think he will do about Savitra's testimony?"

Discouraged now, Patel shook his head. "There are some officials who...let us say, have an association with the Deccan Dholes, one that they would not want to become public. If in the course of his investigation—and yes, I believe he will investigate, at least to some extent—he should turn up any such associations or connections, this would greatly increase the difficulty of his position."

"I have to agree with that assessment," Bombay Sapphire said slowly. "My main concern is for my sister. It may be that she will have to go into hiding, not only from the Dholes and Kallia, but from the Commissioner, the police."

"In fact, a lawsuit may do more harm than good to Sir Edward," Patel mused. "For one thing, it would publicize his involvement."

"If the story is allowed to be printed," sighed Atasi.

Patel nodded. "About that, I may have some influence. The question is, do we go with the story, or do we allow the Commissioner a chance to work in this without publicity, at least for the moment."

Bombay Sapphire glanced around the table. "Why are you all looking to me?" she asked. "I don't..."

"In fact, you *do* decide," Patel said gently. "As you said, you serve Bharat. That has to be the focus for all of us."

Bombay Sapphire considered. Presently she said, "What connection does the *Times* have with the Commissioner's office?" she asked. "Is there some way to find out whether he is investigating, and to what extent?"

"Maury Pawar," said Atasi. "That's his beat. I can brief him quietly on what transpired here, but he will have to be careful with his questions."

"Then I suggest we wait for a few days," said Bombay Sapphire. "After all, Atasi, it will take you at least a day or two to write up the story."

"Humans are interesting," said Daala. The *apsara*-in-training seemed to float to her feet. "Five Guptas, I think, if I may include myself." After Patel's nod, she vanished.

"How is it that you rate your own personal *apsara*?" Patel asked, almost laughing.

"The truth is, I don't yet know what to do with her," said Bombay Sapphire. "But Agni bestowed her upon me for a reason. Besides, I like her company."

"I'm scared," Savitra said suddenly. "I don't know what I'm going to do, I don't..."

"No matter what," said Bombay Sapphire, "I will protect you, *choti*."

Savitra looked at her with wet eyes. "You always have, haven't you?"

"*Hamesha*. Always. Even when I was away, Agni would have warned me if you were in danger."

Savitra began to sob. "I traded you for...for pretty rocks! Oh, Nakushi..."

They hugged. She continued to cry uncontrollably.

"And p-pretty saris, and...and good food, as much as I-I wanted, and..."

"Hush, *choti*."

Daala arrived with the bottles of soda, three orange and two lemon. Unwilling to disturb Bombay Sapphire and Savitra, she distributed them at random. A few minutes seemed to drag into an hour, but at last the two sisters released one another and addressed their beverages. Dayaram Patel handed Savitra a small packet of tissues for her wet eyes.

Bombay Sapphire's face slowly grew serious, somber. "I do not trust Commissioner Rani," she told Patel. "It is not that he is corrupt, but that I cannot take the chance that he is, not where Savitra is concerned. He cannot harm me; the most he can do is make my work a little more difficult." She drew a long breath, and puffed her lips as she exhaled. "I think we have to hide Savitra where she will be safe, very safe." She turned to face Patel as she said this. "Where the police cannot get at her."

"She could be a member of my staff," offered Patel. "But as for hiding if the police should come and want to search the premises...I don't know that she would be safe."

"Temples and shrines, even under Prime Minister Shastri, are still sanctuaries," mused Bombay Sapphire. "But there would be nothing for you to do, Savitra." She considered a moment longer. "Dayaram, will she be safe here for one more day?"

Patel smiled. "I'm sure I can manage that."

"Then if you will excuse me," said Bombay Sapphire, "I have some arrangements to make."

Bombay Sapphire's first arrangement took her straight up for five miles, for that was where the cumulus had formed, preparatory to a squall. She lotused on a cloud and closed her eyes.

"Hear me, O Agni," she whispered.

A long silence followed. She wondered whether Agni were busy preparing the storm to come from the clouds around her. No doubt the god of storms knew what was in her heart and on her mind, and perhaps he did not want to hear her. She calmed herself by whispering a meditative mantra. *"Gati gati paragati parasamgati bodhi svaha."* This she repeated several times before letting it fade into the silence of the clouds.

I know what you will ask, Unwanted One.

The voice of Agni rumbled inside her like soft thunder.

I promise you, your sister will be safe.

"*Sukria*, O Agni. Do you have a task for me?"

When you have completed your arrangement, Doctor Halder has need of you.

Bombay Sapphire rose from her lotus and sped downward. This time at Yawal

Wildlife Sanctuary, she entered through the front door of the administrative building.

Immediately she was recognized. She heard her name whispered in awe, and felt her face warm. She was the servant of Agni, nothing more. But it pleased her to see that because of her these people had hope.

There were three of them in the office: one man and two women. All wore outdoor clothing, as if at any moment they might be called upon to help an animal or deal with the work of a poacher.

A woman stepped forward. The same height as Bombay Sapphire, she was a good ten years older. "I am Gamya Kumar," she said. "I manage this outpost. I must confess, you are one of the last persons I would expect to see here."

Bombay Sapphire smiled easily, and accepted Kumar's hand for a shake. She came directly to the point: her arrangement for Savitra. "No one is to know that she is here," she finished. "You need not concern yourself with her pay; it is not to appear in your budget. Do you understand?" She looked around the front room. "Do you all understand?"

"It shall be as you wish," said Kumar. "Remember us to Agni."

"I shall do so."

Which left a return trip to the estate of Dayaram Patel. Bombay Sapphire's heart stuttered as she reached it: the main building was surrounded by police vehicles. She entered through an open window and cautiously sounded out her surroundings. It was useless to wonder exactly what had transpired, but almost surely the police had come for Savitra. Bombay Sapphire made note of Commissioner Rani, for she felt certain that their paths would cross again one day. In the meantime, where was Savitra? If the police had captured her, they would no longer be at the estate. Worry fretted her as she ran silently along the upper-level hallway, listening for voices.

Listen to your heart.

She had not expected to hear from Agni, but she was immediately obedient. Pausing by an alcove, she keened her ears. *Where are you*, choti? She heard the voice of Dayaram Patel wafting up a staircase. He sounded upset—as he had every right to be. But had the police already found Savitra? No, because Agni would not have told her to listen for her.

Where...?

There were no police on this second level. If they had not yet located Savitra, she must be here somewhere. She twisted, turned, like an antenna seeking a clearer signal. Back the way she had come. Hadn't she noticed a utility closet...?

Yes! There!

She yanked the door open, and right away a mop fell on her. Cleaning equipment and materials, she saw, and two push brooms. But no Savitra...

In the corner, under a great sheet of paper used to protect the floor. Was it moving? She grabbed a corner and yanked the sheet away.

Savitra cried out...

"Hush, *choti*, they'll hear you."

"Na-Nakushi?"

She laughed lightly. "Not at the moment. I'm blue."

"Like a *padme*...a jewel. I remember that first night, when you glowed in the storm..."

She reached out. "Let's get you out of here."

They moved to the window where Bombay Sapphire had entered. Before she could sweep Savitra into her arms, two police officers in white came around the corner of the stairwell. There were no warnings, no commands to halt; they simply opened fire. Bombay Sapphire interposed her body to protect Savitra. There was no way to do this and take off from the window. She would have to fly out with her sister in her arms. Bullets impacted, flattened, and fell clunking to the floor. She dared not wait for them to have to reload. One arm under Savitra's knees, the other behind her shoulders, Bombay Sapphire dove from the window and into the air.

"Are you all right?" yelled Bombay Sapphire. "Are you hit? Did any of those bullets—?"

"I'm fine, I'm fine," cried Savitra. "But they hit *you!*"

Air rushed past them as they rose into the sky. Bombay Sapphire bore east, toward the Sanctuary. She spoke over the wind.

"You have a job," she told Savitra. "You look for and report poaching in Yawal Wildlife Sanctuary."

"But I-I don't know any-anything about..."

"All you have to do is report what you see."

"But the poachers might..."

"Agni will protect you. You will be safe. And Agni will notify me if you need me. Dayaram Patel will send you a weekly pay. The people who run the Sanctuary are expecting you. They'll also have a room for you. This is your chance, *choti.*"

At first Savitra was too stunned to speak. Finally her voice returned. "I don't know what to say. Thank...thank you."

"Almost there."

"Where are you going to be?"

"There is a doctor north of here who needs my help," answered Bombay Sapphire. She did not clarify the job, nor did she mention that Neelam Halder was her lover. "Agni is sending me. I'll find out why after I get there. *Choti*...no one will know you are here. Please keep it that way. The people who run the Sanctuary will also protect you, and say nothing."

"All...all right. But...but what if a cobra or krait...?"

"Agni will protect you. I told you this. There is nothing to fear."

Bombay Sapphire descended, and dropped down in front of the admin building. At first Savitra was wobbly on her feet, but she quickly regained her equilibrium. A banyan tree afforded them partial shade from the overhead sun. The building shone whitely, with just a few grays of shade. The sign over the doorway identified it. The glass door was emblazoned with operating hours.

"Maybe you can guide a tour, too," said Bombay Sapphire.

They stood facing one another. "I wish I knew...I wish...," said Savitra.

They hugged; quaking, Savitra wept.

"You have always been, and always will be, my sister," Bombay Sapphire whispered fiercely into her ear.

Savitra sniffed, and wiped her nose on a blue shoulder. She gave a little nod in final acknowledgement. "So we start over?"

Bombay Sapphire shook her head. "We pick up where we left off."

"Oh, yes."

"I have to go, *choti*. I'll stop by when I can."

In parting, they kissed cheeks.

Flying away, Bombay Sapphire wondered whether her tears were blue.

012

The great Himalayas loomed ahead in the distance. Already at an altitude of four miles, Bombay Sapphire still flew well below the tallest peaks. Near the foothills off to her left spread the small town of Kamet, her destination. Gradually, like a Spitfire peeling off with its squadron toward the target, she swooped closer to the forested surface with the patchwork of glades and small savannahs. Kamet lay a mile distant as she landed. For a few moments she debated whether to transform to her human self. But many of the people of Kamet knew her as Bombay Sapphire, and she had no reason to conceal that identity from them. Even Maryam, the nurse at Halder's clinic, had come to appreciate her.

Nevertheless, she elected to walk into the town, rather than fly. During this journey, she acquired an entourage of small, half-naked children who wanted nothing more from her than a short flight in her arms. She resisted for a while, but in the end she succumbed to the plaintive begging, and—holding two at a time—took them on short, low flights. When these ended, they followed her into Kamet.

The afternoon was late. The clinic was treating its last scheduled patient. The children, seeing that she had a specific destination in mind, dispersed after she went inside. The receptionist, a new hire whose whites glowed even in the late sunlight through the front window, was startled at first to see her, even though Bombay Sapphire had no doubt that Neelam Halder had advised the girl that she might stop by, now and then.

What Halder did not mention—because he did not know—was that an *apsara*-in-training might pop in beside Bombay Sapphire at any moment. A high-pitched cry pierced the air, and the girl at the desk almost passed out. But she steadied herself soon enough, and recovered much of her composure.

"Are you," she began, addressing Daalachini, "are you a new patient?"

"Perhaps I have made a mistake," sighed Daala. She straightened her diaphanous violet sari, which had become askew during her materialization. "But I am in training."

Bombay Sapphire reassured her with a touch to her shoulder. "I won't tell Agni if you won't."

Daala managed a light and nervous laugh. "I am certain that he knows."

Bombay Sapphire pointed to the intercom on the desk. "Would you please tell Doctor Halder that a woman has suffered enough snow to turn her blue, and seeks the attention of a medic?"

The girl, whose name tag read Hansa, or Swan, relayed the message, but changed the ending to, "Seeks medical attention."

"That is not quite what I said," Bombay Sapphire told her.

"I-I...," said Hansa, and made the correction.

Moments later, Neelam Halder entered the lobby and came to a halt. Daala said, "This must be my cue," and vanished.

Bombay Sapphire smiled easily. For now, all was right in her world.

After Halder changed out of his medical whites and Bombay Sapphire transformed, they walked to a small restaurant closer to the center of Kamet. "You do not appear to be very chilled," he observed along the way.

"I believe the cure is shared body warmth," she told him, masking a grin. She was now wearing simple tan slacks and a white blouse, and sandals.

"I'll just check *Grey's Anatomy* on that."

He held the door for her, but led the way to a table by the front window. They were attended immediately by an adolescent girl who offered them menus, which they declined.

"Tikka masala for two," Halder told her. "Bowls of rice. And green tea to drink, with lemon."

The girl hurried off. Nakushi said, "I haven't been to this place, but that girl looks familiar."

"She's one of those you rescued from that avalanche."

"I'm glad she found work, but she should still be in school."

"She graduates next year, I believe." He reached out for her hand. "Nakushi..."

She nodded. "Me, too." She sobered. "Agni wanted me here. I do not know why."

"I was afraid of that."

She squeezed his hand, and released it. "I think he also sent me here because he knew I wanted to be with you. He must have read my mind."

"I know. But I am not anxious to have to deal with a humanitarian disaster."

"It may not come to that."

The tea arrived, steaming from its mugs. Each had a wedge of lemon alongside on the saucer. She prepared hers and waited for Halder. When he was ready, they lifted their mugs.

"Tonight," she said, and sipped. It was all she needed to say.

During the meal she brought him up to date on her sister and on fighting poachers. When she reached the part about Sir Edward Willoughby, he laid down his spoon and stared at her.

"What?" she said, interrupting her own narrative.

"I heard something about that," he told her. "Abandoned in the snow near a monastery?"

"This time," she said. "If there is a next time, I'll leave him in Siberia. There's plenty of snow, but not many monasteries."

"I don't understand why he would involve himself."

"And I did not ask," said Nakushi. "He was there, he was..."

The tea in the mug began to tremble. When it began to slosh over the rim of the mug, Nakushi said, "*Ashmita.*" Transformed, Bombay Sapphire shot to her feet. "Everyone go outside now. It's an earthquake."

Halder was already right beside her, helping to usher the few diners and staff out to the streets. A window cracked. A beam fell, and Bombay Sapphire caught it. The quaking threatened to spill Halder. She picked him up and rose a couple feet off the floor, where the trembling could not affect them. They were the last ones to leave the restaurant.

Outside reigned havoc and fear, punctuated by screams and shouts of alarm. Already several of the rude dwellings were collapsing, amid shattered windows and crumpled roofs. Somewhere in Kamet, a siren sounded. Plumes of agitated dust soon rose into the air and enveloped the damage. Rumbling, followed by heavy but muffled impacts, announced the distant fall of boulders from the mountains. Bombay

Sapphire and Halder began searching the crumbled houses for survivors, even though the quake had not yet subsided. The dust made Halder cough; she could not help him.

Magically, Daala appeared beside her. Bombay Sapphire did not hesitate. "Get as many people out of the houses as you can. Can you be hurt?"

The question puzzled Daala. She shook her head as she flew off.

"Be careful anyway," Bombay Sapphire called after her.

Across the street, Maryam and Hansa had already begun to tend to the injured, most of whom seemed to be the children who had escorted Bombay Sapphire to Kamet. Wood splintered nearby; a tree had shattered. She shot toward it, catching it before it struck two of the children. With her strength, it was almost no effort at all to shove the tree away, where it could harm no one.

"Maryam," she called. "Hansa. Get the children out into the street where they won't be struck by debris."

A vehicle careened along the street, the woman driving it either frightened or hurt. Bombay Sapphire flew to it and yanked the door off to pull the woman free and onto the street. Moving onto the vacated seat, she shifted to neutral, slammed on the brakes, and turned off the ignition. The woman clutched at the vehicle, sobbing now.

"My husband," she cried. "If he sees what I've done to his car..."

For that problem, Bombay Sapphire felt helpless. None of her powers enabled her to deal with marital relationships. She could only console the woman with a pat on the shoulder, and move on to the next danger...

And the next...

And the next...

It was a long night, and not the kind of long night she had hoped for.

The earthquake had subsided after perhaps three minutes, but people continued to cry out with each aftershock. Kamet itself was in ruins. Halder's clinic had survived, but barely. The X-ray machine and most of the other equipment still functioned, and the emergency generator had kicked in. But all the windows had been broken, a portion of the roof had collapsed, and the front door dangled by one hinge.

"We'll worry about the damage later," Bombay Sapphire told him. "Let's get people treated first."

Her presence seemed to galvanize him into action. As Maryam and Hansa returned with several victims in tow, he began to issue instructions in his doctor's voice—confident and reassuring. Bombay Sapphire, who had previous medical experience with Halder, knew what needed to be done without having to be told. Bandages, antiseptic, gauze, X-ray plates—she brought him whatever was needed.

The treatments seemed endless. Tens of people arrived at the clinic, for it was the only one in Kamet. Some had already been treated with makeshift bandaging. Some had the million-mile stares that signified a state of shock. Evidently Hansa had more than secretarial training, for she was adept at treating some of the minor injuries.

After an hour or so, the other two women on the clinic's nursing staff arrived. They had a few bruises, and a cut or two that had already received its dark orange line of mercurochrome. Understandably, they had been shaken. But they went to work with calm deliberation.

Bombay Sapphire lost count of the patients. Upwards of sixty, she guessed. A few stragglers were trickling in, the last of the survivors. The Red Cross still had yet to arrive, and she pointed this out to Halder.

He was bent over a patient, excising a shard of wood from his left calf. "This isn't the only town that was hit," he told her. "Kamet would be an after-thought. There simply aren't enough responders to deal with everything."

She peered at him. "Are you all right?"

"I will be better when I've finished."

That, she thought, might be a while.

013

Kallia, the black demon and avatar of Shiva, hurled a plate at the wall. Ceramic fragments rained down on Sanjiv, who was sitting in a chair against that wall. He shivered, but dared not dodge them. A gaunt youth of eighteen, he had just delivered his report on Savitra.

"She could not have removed those bars or the stones," growled Kallia. "Someone else did it: the blue witch. Savitra was supposed to have remained in jail until she understood the meaning of fear." Without mirth she smiled at Sanjiv. "The way you understand it."

He nodded emphatically.

"She must be found. Put all our resources on it. Half a million rupees to whoever locates her. Spread the word."

Sanjiv gaped at her, uncertain.

"Go!" she shrieked.

After Sanjiv fled, Kallia sat down at her desk and leaned back, eyes fixed on the repairs in the ceiling, where Bombay Sapphire had flown through during an earlier escape. Hated seethed inside the demon. The blue witch was not merely an adversary, to be bought off or beaten; she was a nemesis.

Her phone rang. She let it ring five times before she picked it up. She did not speak.

"You know who this is," said the man. "We have been given extensive details of all the operations of the Deccan Dholes. I can make those details disappear, but it will be costly."

Shocked by the revelation, Kallia spoke impetuously. "I don't care what it costs," she said. "Do it. Now, where is the blue witch? Where is Savitra?"

After a moment's hesitation, the caller said, "There was a serious earthquake in Uttar Pradesh, centered around Etawah. She goes where there is trouble. She may be there now."

"And Savitra?"

"I know you have people on it. I will add some, but I cannot weaken security and enforcement."

Kallia clenched her jaws and gritted out her response. "I understand. Report when you have something."

She rang off without another word.

* * *

Savitra was given a white pith helmet bearing the logo of the Yawal Wildlife Sanctuary and a flare gun, and instructed to fire the flare if she came across any activity that violated the sanctuary protocols. She was also given a first-aid kit, attached to a green canvas belt alongside a hunting knife and a canteen. The kit included antivenin. Not that she would need such a shot—she was fully protected by Agni—but she might come across someone who had been bitten.

She had also been given three hours of first-aid training, so that she might help visitors in distress. Finally, she had a map of the sanctuary that delineated her area of responsibility, and a compass, although the latter was most useful if you knew your location in relation to the admin office.

Alone now in the humidity and heat of the jungle—already her khaki outfit was sweat-stained—she marveled at the job she was to do. It occurred to her that as the head of the Deccan Dholes, she had mostly told others what to do; now, as an employee of the YWS, she actually got to *do*. Primarily, she wandered and listened. The jungle always spoke; one simply had to have the right ear to hear it. She was open to learning the language. Right away she noticed that it fell silent wherever she passed, and picked up again after she had moved on. Perhaps she would take some getting used to.

A snake slithered across her path; a python no longer than she was tall. It seemed not to notice her, even though she had paused to let it finish crossing. She thought she should feel revulsion, but found herself curious instead. The python might have been hunting small game. Here she laughed lightly: python poaching. A wry smile crossed her face as she decided not to fire the flare.

Something heavy was moving through the trees ahead of her. Saplings snapped and dry leaves crunched. Unlikely it was a predator, Savitra concluded, for it was making noise that would frighten prey. An elephant, perhaps? Not an adult, possibly a yearling. She continued to look in the direction of the sound; now it seemed to be crossing her path. Even as she peered between the tree trunks ahead, she thought to detect movement.

And there it was: a rhinoceros, gray and with the distinctive folded skin. This one was young, perhaps barely a yearling. Now it turned to follow the game path—the same path Savitra was standing on. She froze; she did not know whether to move or to hold still. On it came, as if it had yet to notice her. Some three paces away it finally halted, now aware of an impediment to its journey.

It snorted.

Very slowly Savitra bent and tore free a tuft of grass. Even as the fear of what-am-I-doing! crossed her mind, she extended her hand and offered the grass. Her heart pounded. Never had she been this close to such an animal. It was not quite shoulder-high on her, but must have weighed half a ton. If it charged...but Agni would protect her. The rhino came forward, step by step, seeming to sniff the air. Its thick lips struck the grass. It opened its mouth to reveal sharp incisors and tusks. Gently it took the grass from her and began to chew. And all the while, Savitra held her breath.

Afraid that any kind of movement now might cause the rhino to run away or toward her, she kept her arm extended. Her ribs ached, a reminder to take a breath. The rhino continued to chew...and then it stopped. Its tiny eyes regarded her. Taking one more step, it nudged her hand with its horn.

"More?" whispered Savitra. "You want more?"

She bent and picked another sheaf, and offered it. Again the rhino took it from her. She watched while it chewed. It was tempting to rub the beast's horn, and after girding herself with a deep breath, she caressed its face with her fingertips. The rhino did not stop chewing, nor did it mind the contact.

She was about to feed it a third clump when abruptly it bolted, brushing past her without harming her. It fled along the path, for the trees were too thick for it to penetrate into the safety of the jungle. Instinct took over Savitra: if the rhino had reason to run away, so might she. She eased back into the trees, where the natural sounds had silenced. Still she heard something crashing through the vegetation. From her vantage point behind a thick trunk she peered around and spied three men, one with a large rifle.

"Gods, no!" she breathed.

She dodged back before they noticed her. Silently she exhorted the rhino to run, get away, as fast as you can. She took mental notes. The two unarmed men were native, perhaps trackers. They preceded a white man who carried the rifle. Like her, he was in khakis; a yellow pith helmet covered his head. His hair was white, and he looked old enough to be her grandfather. The trio rushed past her; she heard a metallic sound as the white man chambered a round in the rifle.

"No...," she moaned.

The men soon disappeared around a bend in the path. Savitra stepped out into the sunlight and fired her flare gun so that the flare might arc over the admin office. Immediately afterwards, a shot sent birds into the air, squawking. A second shot galvanized her. Rifle or no rifle, she had to run and...

Savitra was unable to complete the thought. Anger and her gorge rose together. Not my rhino, she pleaded as she raced along the path. Please not my rhino. Thin branches scratched her bare arms as she ran, and clutched at her clothing. She rounded the bend in the path...and skidded to a halt on the grass.

Already the rhino lay on the ground, unmoving. Its nose was a bloody mess, and the horn was gone. One of the trackers was holding a cloth bag that leaked blood.

Savitra screamed.

As the men turned toward her, she loaded another flare into the gun. The white man, realizing what she was about, started to bring his rifle to bear. Savitra fired first; the flare struck him in the center of his khaki shirt and ignited it. His hoarse screams redounded throughout the jungle.

The two trackers turned and fled.

As the man's screaming faded to moans of extreme pain, Savitra approached. Already she had loaded her third and last flare. One closer look told her the rhino was dead. She knelt down beside the man. The shirt still smoldered, and the flare was burning a hole through him. Pale eyes filled with agony gaped up at her as she inspected the wound with the detachment of a surgeon. She did not unplug the flare. The man's eyes began to dull.

"Die," she said, with utter calm. His eyes closed. He did not draw another breath.

Savitra got back to her feet and wiped her eyes on the short sleeve of her shirt. This did not stop the crying, nor did she expect it to. More than anything else at this moment, she wished Nakushi were here. She needed to be held.

Half an hour later, Savitra entered the admin office. The three people within stared at her, aghast. Before anyone could speak, she said, "From now on, I carry a pistol. And I would like a rifle as well, but I shall require training with it."

The younger of the two women spoke. "What," she cried, "happened?"

Her eyes still refusing to dry, Savitra told them.

* * *

The rescue work was exhausting. At first, Bombay Sapphire reverted to Nakushi, to avoid unwanted attention, but she soon tired of all that had to be done, and because blue once more. If Bombay Sapphire was not indefatigable, she was the closest thing to it.

From time to time she returned to the clinic to see whether Neelam Halder needed her. Each time, although the front room was clotted with the injured, the staff seemed to be coping. Each time, then, she returned to the collapsed houses, the shattered buildings, the toppled trees, searching for movement and keen to all sounds. A whimper drew her toward a flattened hovel. Approaching, she spotted a small bare arm: a child had been trapped under the rubble. Other movement caught her eye: Daala the apsara-in-training, attired now in a yellow tunic and loose-fitting white pants, had come to join her in the rescue effort.

Together they lifted the wall that had fallen on the child—a little boy of about eight years old. His face was bloody; a splinter, or perhaps a nail, had jabbed his left cheek. His right leg was bent at an angle that made Bombay Sapphire wince in sympathy. Daala removed more debris, while Bombay Sapphire determined how to lift the boy without further injuring him.

"I wish we had a stretcher," she muttered to herself.

Daala snapped her fingers, and a stretcher appeared on the dirt beside the boy.

Gently they lifted him onto the stretcher, and each took an end. "I didn't know apsaras were capable of that kind of magic," Bombay Sapphire called over her shoulder to her.

"Several skills were bestowed on me by Agni when he assigned me to you," Daala replied. "In truth, however, it was Agni who supplied this stretcher."

"What skills?"

"Flight, for one."

"I thought apsaras *could* fly."

"We can barely flutter and hover," Daala told her. "But we dance well."

At the entrance to the clinic, Bombay Sapphire turned around and backed her way inside. There was no room anywhere on the floor to put him, so they laid the stretcher on the registration counter. While Daala stood over him, Bombay Sapphire went to the operating room at the back of the clinic and found Halder there, just finishing up.

After briefing him, she found time for a few breaths. Not that her lungs needed the air, but she needed a moment or two. Halder patted her on the shoulder and went to examine the new patient. Daala soon joined her.

"As far as I can tell," said the apsara-in-training, "we've rescued all the living. But there are about a hundred bodies that will require cremation. Some have been released to the families. Others..." She shrugged helplessly. "It is difficult for me to convince myself that the bodies are nothing more than containers for the essence. Perhaps that is why, after a thousand years, I still require training."

"When you become dispassionate or detached, you lose something of your humanity," said Bombay Sapphire.

Daalachini smiled. "You may not have noticed, but I am not human."

"You could have fooled me, Daala."

"You are kind to say so. This despite your background, when you might have become embittered."

Bombay Sapphire laughed. "Agni talks too much."

"This is not so," said Daala, aghast at the thought. "I was assigned by Agni to watch you from the moment of your birth."

"Fate," murmured Bombay Sapphire. "Destiny. Of course Agni would have known all the moments of my life, and would intervene at the most propitious moment."

"The gods do not often intervene, Nakushi. Suffering is inevitable because life is hard. It was never intended to be otherwise. An example of this suffering is East Pakistan. Fifty thousand people die in the floods each year, yet people continue to live there. Still, now and then ways are found to ease that suffering. Thus the work that you do."

"Are you sure you're still in training?"

"Perhaps, not after my time with you, Nakushi. The gods know what has happened, what is happening, and what will happen, because it is all happening at the same time. It is only to the physical universe that the very concept of time and its passage applies. We apsaras are involved only in those moments as humans are aware of their passing."

"My actions are more mundane," said Bombay Sapphire. "I serve Agni in the physical world. In *this* world. I am not concerned with the next world, unless he so orders it."

"Agni did say that you have little formal education," said the apsara-in-training.

"Agni gives me the knowledge to do the things I do to serve him," she said. "I retain this knowledge even after I transform back to...my human self." She stood up straight. "Let's see what else we can do here."

The lights went out. People wailed in shock and in fear. Bombay Sapphire rushed into the front room, with Daala flying beside her. "Neelam," she called out, and barely perceived his shadowy outline at the registration counter.

"Over here."

While Daala moved to comfort the children and the fearful, Bombay Sapphire joined Halder at the counter. Needing light, she snapped her fingers. Instantly a great spark illuminated the entire front room. It hung in the air like a strange Hindu spirit. Wide-eyed faces stared at it, at first in disbelief, then in reverence. Daala held a child in her arms.

"I don't know how you do that," said Halder. "But thank you."

"I don't know how I do it, either," she said. "How can I help?"

"I need to see where I'm sewing."

Again she snapped her fingers, and a smaller spark hovered a couple feet above the wound he was closing. With nothing more for her to do there, she began to wander about the front room. A touch here, a few soft words there, a caress now and then, all served to quell fears. Obviously she was some sort of benevolent goddess, and as long as she was present, no further harm might befall any of them.

The night hung around like a shroud, lit only by sparks. Outside they heard the grinding of heavy machinery, as vehicles arrived from elsewhere to clear debris. But reconstruction could begin only after daybreak.

Eventually Halder's legs wobbled as he moved around, treating what he could. He resisted when Bombay Sapphire drew him aside.

"If you fall down, you cannot help anyone," she told him. "Sit for a moment. Gather yourself. Daala will see to the first aid. I will see to splints and bandages."

"Nakushi..."

Her smile eased his worries. "I'm glad to be here, with you."

Cries of pain and distress gradually subsided. She set a broken arm, and cleaned and bandaged several gashes caused by wood splintered in the earthquake. Daala wielded a pitcher of water while Bombay Sapphire held the few drinking glasses that were on hand.

Finally dawn arrived, and the sun returned to the horizon. The electricity was still out, but no one cared at the moment. For the time being, their plight had been eased. Bombay Sapphire and Halder sought the comfort of the bench outside the entrance, and let the morning sun warm them. His white smock was a mess of various shades of red and smudged with dust and dirt. He removed it and folded it and set it aside, all with concentrated deliberation, as if he were healing his clothing. Bombay Sapphire slid closer, until their flanks pressed against one another.

"Do you want me to transform?" she asked him.

Halder slipped an arm around her shoulders. "Yes, but no," he replied sadly. "I'm tired."

"Then I shall hold you."

"That I would—"

Suddenly Bombay Sapphire threw her head back and arched her spine. Blue eyes whitened as they rolled up under her eyelid. Her entire body trembled, but not with pain. She uttered no sound save one long gasp.

Just as quickly the paroxysm subsided. Recovered, she sat up straight, then gained her feet.

"What is it this time?" Halder worried, having witnessed her endure this before.

"My sister," she croaked. "My sister. Savitra. She's accused..." She swallowed hard, and tried again. "She's been accused of murdering Sir Edward Willoughby."

Bombay Sapphire will return in Episode #6 in 2024.

www.ingramcontent.com/pod-product-compliance
Lightning Source LLC
LaVergne TN
LVHW010341070526
838199LV00065B/5765